DIE,
DECORATOR,
DIE

A NOVEL OF MURDER,
GREED AND INTERIOR DESIGN

FRANKLIN H. LEVY

DIE, DECORATOR, DIE

A NOVEL OF MURDER, GREED AND INTERIOR DESIGN

ISBN-10: 1-59777-591-6
ISBN-13: 978-1-59777-591-5
Library of Congress Cataloging-In-Publication Data Available

Book Design by: Sonia Fiore

Printed in the United States of America

Phoenix Books, Inc.
9465 Wilshire Boulevard, Suite 840
Beverly Hills, CA 90212

10 9 8 7 6 5 4 3 2 1

To my wife Lynda,
who told me to publish or perish.

PROLOGUE

Megan slid her Neiman's credit card into the cellar door lock. The house on Beacon Hill had been empty for over a year and she was hoping for minimal security. The lock clicked and the door opened. She kissed her Neiman's card, whispering, "You've never let me down," as she dropped it back into her satchel and took out a flashlight. The house was dark, but she was able to find her way up the back stairs. Lacking any sense of humor, she failed to see how absurd this situation might appear to a bystander: a woman in a black Chanel suit breaking into a house carrying a twelve-thousand-dollar Hermes purse.

Shining her light, Megan walked into the living room. The light beam bounced off the walls as she looked around. The room was cavernous and the clicking of her Manolo Blahnik heels echoed as she paced. She touched the wood paneling that ran halfway up one wall, trailing her hand across the wood as she moved. While she looked and roamed, she imagined how the room would look as a future cover for *Traditional Homes* or *Architectural Digest*.

I've already made myself rich, she thought, *and now it's time to be famous.* Megan had no illusions about her place in Boston's decorating hierarchy. She used social connections to meet women with more money than taste.

Then she relied on her good looks to get their husbands thinking about how she tasted. Sealing a deal was one thing, but a Show House success would finally make her legit. Consultants from New York had already been promised cash bonuses if her designs—that is, the ones they did for her—were chosen. Her competition, the other designers, wouldn't get to look at the house until the next day. She wanted to leave very little to chance.

Balancing her flashlight on the fireplace mantle, she walked around the room, taping pieces of wallpaper onto the walls and dropping fabric on the floor. A fine chintz caught her eye and she caressed the fabric before dropping it. She loved luxury and fine things. She ran her hands down the sides of her pants, luxuriating in herself— expensive clothes covering liposuctioned limbs. She was so lost in thought that she was not really listening. Had she been, she might have heard the sound of someone's bare feet tiptoeing up behind her. She might even have heard the rustle of cloth. But she heard nothing.

However, even the intensity of her scheming had not completely disabled her sense of touch. Her last waking sensation was the feeling of someone wrapping fabric around her head and jerking her around, toward the beam of the flashlight. More puzzled than shocked, she stared at the light and thought: *I've never seen that pattern before*, as a hammer crashed down on her head.

ONE

"Call me Ishmael!"

It was starting again. The dream. There was Ishmael Partagas, a drug dealer I had represented, waving to me from the deck of the QE II. At his trial, I had been able to suppress evidence and thus assure his acquittal. I knew that as a player in one of the world's worst games, he would best serve society by engaging in enforced and solitary introspection in the big house for the next twenty years. But there he was sailing off into the sunset, and I was sitting in a single crew shell in the middle of the ocean, waving to him and hoping that he would call me again.

I started rowing. I had actually never rowed before. The closest I had come to a shell was leaning against one with a drink in hand at a cocktail party at the Harvard boathouse. The boat seemed incredibly narrow and cramped, and I couldn't imagine how the rowers kept from tipping over on each stroke. The thought of my actually sitting in one and rowing seemed absurd at the time. So my present predicament seemed very unusual. Especially when I saw (as I always did in the dream) that my boat had been decorated. The inside ribs of the shell were covered with undulating moiré wallpaper. My seat had a cushion that was color-coordinated with the wallpaper and was watermarked in plaid to play off the paper. Whoever had decorated the boat had also added a couple of dangling ties. Although a nice decorative touch, they were in danger of tangling with the rowing mechanism. The oarlocks were antique wall brackets and the hull had a fleur-de-lis pattern painted on it.

I was rowing like crazy but making very little progress. This could be explained by the fact that the entire body of water was on an incline and I was rowing uphill. I wondered if anyone was watching and, if so, what they thought of this rather overdone seagoing Sisyphus. Things seemed strange. Ben-Hur had it easier. But maybe I was going upstream to spawn and would be rewarded for my labors. I smiled and rowed onward.

As I was struggling up the watery incline, things started passing me, as they always did, in the other direction. The first person I saw was Fay Fine. She was an old divorce client whose husband was still paying through the nose. She was sitting on something that looked like Cleopatra's Barge—the one at Caesar's Palace in Las Vegas. Twelve slaves were pulling at the oars, while another fed her peeled grapes. As we got closer, I could see that all the slaves had the same face as her husband. Our boats passed and she looked over at me.

"Thanks, Buzz," she said. "I knew when you attached his safe deposit boxes and threatened him with the IRS my little Finsky would come back to me." One of the slaves looked up and she kicked him. "Keep rowing, Finsky."

As they continued on down the river, I heard her calling, "You're a great lawyer, Buzz." And as she faded out of sight I heard in the distance, "A great lawyer...a great lawyer...."

She was gone and I set to rowing with new fury, although I made no progress.

Something big was approaching from the other

direction. As it closed in, I could see that it was a large flat barge, the kind associated with pictures of coal, or scrap, or garbage. It was empty except for four men sitting around a table. They were all dressed in tacky but expensive cruise wear and were playing gin rummy. I knew them. They were all old clients—two real estateniks and two garmentos. They had done a joint venture deal together building a string of factory outlet clothing stores. The real estateniks would build; the garmentos would operate. However, the partners had been so busy altering invoices, destroying records, and pocketing cash that they'd missed a few payments to their banks and had ended up personally on the hook for millions of dollars. Their good fortune was that I had organized them and their businesses as a series of Delaware limited partnerships, with general partners incorporated in Nevada, whose bearer shares were held by a law firm in Panama. Their good fortune was the banks' bad luck. These pillars of the community were able to settle for pennies.

As their barge lumbered past, they put down their cards and stood up waving at me. "Buzzy," one of them yelled, "you're a genius! You saved us *and* our money. Look, we're floating down to Boca. Maybe you'll stop by—a little golf, a little food, maybe even a little broad." They emitted a vulgar group chortle. "We love ya, baby. You really fucked those banks, Buzzy. You're a great lawyer." And as they floated off into the distance, I could hear them yelling in unison, "You're a great lawyer...a great lawyer...a great lawyer."

Even as I slept, I knew I was sweating, tossing and turning, troubled by the theme that was emerging. All I could do was pull faster in an attempt to escape. But my progress was the same as before, which is to say nil. In the distance coming toward me I saw a Boston Whaler with a tall man standing at the wheel. As it neared, I could see that the man was wearing a suit and carrying a valise. If this was Ben on his way to Africa, I was jumping ship and abandoning dream. But as he got closer, I could see his three-piece suit, his pocket watch, his wrinkled mien. I knew who he was.

"Oh my God," I exclaimed, "you're Clarence Darrow."

"Cut the God crap, Levin. I'm a famous atheist, even if this does appear to be the afterlife."

"Mr. Darrow, you've got to help me. You're the greatest lawyer who ever lived. I'm sitting here rowing, getting nowhere. If any more old clients come by and remind me why they think I'm so good I'm going to jump. How can I be like you?"

"You're a lawyer, Levin. You want to be like me. It's easy. Just keep winning. No one remembers a brilliant loser with a social conscience. Be a winner. Every case is the seventh game of the World Series. Either win, or, in the words of your la-dee-da Whiffenpoofs, 'pass and be forgotten with the rest.' You got that, boy?"

"Yes sir."

"And Levin," he said as his boat pulled away. "Do you really want to be a great lawyer?"

"Yes sir."

"Then, Levin," he intoned as his boat moved off into the distance, "Get paid...get paid...get paid."

And he was gone.

I felt that I was waking up, that consciousness was creeping in. Usually I woke from the dream with a feeling of general unease. Was I subconsciously sending myself a message about the state of my life? Misdirection, right direction, career choices, the price of winning—who knew? Or maybe I had crossed over: Was it really Clarence Darrow?

Instead of the usual cold sweat, this time I noticed a decidedly warm glow spreading up and down my body.

Unless I was very much mistaken, a tongue was circling the inner portions of my outer ear. I reached over and pulled a familiar and delightfully naked body in closer. "What a nice surprise," I whispered.

"You know me," said Ally. "You only have to ask once."

"What does that mean?" I asked, wondering why I'd chosen this magic moment to strike up a superfluous conversation.

"Are you kidding?" she said. "I'm lying here sound asleep and I wake to my own husband mumbling, 'Get laid, get laid, get laid.' And I say to myself, 'How sweet, he's having an erotic dream.' But then I think, *what if it's not about me?* So, you see," Ally continued, her voice trailing off as it worked its way down my chest, "you really leave a girl no choice."

As I lay back smiling the smile of the soon-to-be satisfied, I rejoiced in the fact that the innocent misinterpretation of just one consonant can have such a stupendous result. I even started to whistle the old Rod Stewart standard, "Some Guys Have All The Luck." Then, and only then, with a sound more resonant than any shot heard round the world, did the alarm go off. It was heads up for the Levins. A new day was dawning.

TWO

We had been on vacation for two weeks, teasingly almost long enough to break old Pavlovian habits. One last gentle caress and then unlock, unload, and into the shower. At least the shower massage was still throbbing, and I aimed a cold and fast stream right between my eyes. I hummed reveille and tried to think of some mental trick to wake myself up. Of all 6 a.m. alarms, the unkindest was the first one after Labor Day. Goodbye, Beach Boys. Hello, "September Song."

The cold spray hit me face on, sparking a daydream far more pleasant than the "dream" of last night. There I was standing knee deep in the surf at Nantucket's Great Point, casting for the last bluefish of summer. The water pounded against me and I opened my eyes with exhilaration. That was a mistake. Not salt mist but dribbles of dandruff shampoo washed into my eyes. I fled the shower feeling for a towel. Rubbing my eyes, I looked into the mirror. Yikes—look at that paunch. No wonder my bathing suit felt tighter at the end of the summer than in the beginning. I sucked in my stomach and looked again, this time more charitably. Maybe I didn't look too bad for a post-middle-aged lawyer. I had most of my curly blond hair.

Enough shampoo had run into my eyes so that the blue still sparkled. At least I hadn't gotten any shorter yet.

My reverie was interrupted by two voices down the hall.

"Dad, where's my shirt?"

"Buzz, is there any coffee?"

Maybe I should buy a Stairmaster. Or a rowing machine. I could start walking eighteen holes instead of taking a cart.

"Dad, help! I've got to get to school."

"Coffee. I need coffee."

One last look in the mirror. This was a problem that needed some thought. Perhaps some study. But these were issues for another day. As for today, everything was coming up eights: the eighth of September, and the eighth grade was about to begin. But not without a shirt.

"Hang on, guys!" I yelled. "Your hero is coming."

I entered Justin's room and found him with that familiar look of bewilderment. He had just found his pants, was holding a necktie, and was anxiously awaiting the arrival of a shirt. The summer had been much better to him than it had to me. Two months at camp in New Hampshire, finished off with three weeks in Nantucket, had produced a first class beach boy look right here in the heart of Newton, Massachusetts. Some people say we look alike. I wish. He was already my height with a face that would melt a grandmother's heart. Considering all of the cheek pinching he's suffered over the years, I am always amazed at the absence of permanent facial bruising.

"Hey, sport," I suggested, "have you tried the back of the closet?" I opened the door and pushed back a dozen pairs of khaki pants to reveal a year's supply of button downs *avec* ponies.

"Who put them there?" asked Justin. I hoped he would have more success locating the hypotenuse of a triangle than his clothes.

I left his room and ran downstairs to the kitchen, greeted by the smell of fresh coffee wafting up from the combination automatic bean grinder/coffeemaker. Say what you want about Yuppies, they're definitely responsible for a lot of great kitchen gadgets. Two thousand years from now some archeologist will no doubt unearth the remains of a Williams Sonoma store, where, after much study, it will be classified a holy place at which the natives stood in long lines to worship the greatest accomplishments of their primitive civilization.

I grabbed two cups and walked back up to the wonderful spot where only minutes before I had awakened with such hope.

"I'm not ready for summer to end," said Allyn, arching her body under the pink, handmade patchwork quilt that went so well with the faux headboard cleverly painted on the wall.

"You?" I exclaimed. "What about me? One day back and I'm already paddling up the river in a shell to legal Palookaville."

"Oh no, Buzz. Not the dream again."

"Oh, yes. I tell you, Ally, I think I'm going through a mid-law crisis. It's Diogenes time. I'm going to grab a lantern, wrap myself in a sheet and wander through the streets of Boston looking for a man who's honest."

"What'll you do when you find him?"

"You kidding? I'll represent him."

"Forget it, Buzz. Honest men don't need lawyers. You'll just have to think of something else."

I looked down at Ally, still curled in the sheets. I thought of something else. Slightly dejected and mildly erected, I did some quick calculations based on the folds and wrinkles in the sheets and planted my head in the spot where I determined I was most likely to strike gold.

"Ouch!" I exclaimed as she delivered several noogies to my head. "Is this the way Nora Charles treated Nick?"

"She had Asta to protect her. You wouldn't buy me a dog," said Ally, conveniently forgetting the dog I had once brought home, to no one's delight—including the dog's.

Our witty repartee and head bashing came to an end when Justin called up from the kitchen, "Where's breakfast?"

"Call Maria," I yelled down, still harboring some deluded hope of a quickie.

"She's still asleep," responded Justin.

Who was I kidding? No quickie, no hope, no Maria.

Maria is another story. Let me set the record straight by stating that I always wanted to be a successful lawyer, married to a successful career woman, with all the meaningless materialistic trappings that accompany the American dream. However, I do take some pride in the fact that I still have a soul. It wasn't so long ago that I was a liberal (almost radical) college student marching, parading, and wearing love beads. Despite my youthful and idealistic determination to build a new society, there were certain contradictions in my personal dialectic. For example, after surrounding the White House and demanding Nixon be evicted, my friends and I would walk over to Georgetown to have dinner at La Rive Gauche, because that's where Jackie O had once hung out. While I always knew I'd stay true to the liberal agenda, personal suffering was not part of the program.

Because Allyn and I both worked, we needed an au pair, and that was Maria. Maria was from Mexico, and to assuage my conscience, I convinced myself that she was a political exile from Chiapas where her father was a subcommandante leading the native resistance. Actually, she was the only child of the former Treasurer of the State of Chiapas. She had come to the United States to study horseback riding at a nearby women's junior college. Her education had been interrupted when, at the first sounds of an uprising, her father had disappeared along with much of the local treasury. While awaiting word of her father or some clue to the access code of his numbered Swiss accounts, Maria had answered our ad in the paper. She was the only answer we received, and soon she was another spoiled only child living in our house. Personally, I had very high hopes for her father's resurrection.

I arrived in the kitchen, followed by Allyn. We managed to find some cereal and milk for the kid, and more coffee for ourselves. Like any good sitcom family, we took our accustomed places in the breakfast room. This room, like the rest of the house, had been brought to us by the interior design skills of Allyn Levin: wife, mother, and professional decorator. A few months ago, the room, minus us, had been on the front cover of a national magazine featuring kitchen makeovers. The rest of the house had been in other magazines. I had well-known walls and famous furniture, a formal living room, an English dining room, an elegantly simple den—*c'est moi.*

It wasn't always *moi.* When Ally and I first met, I was a struggling attorney living in a high-rise on Boston's waterfront. My furnishings consisted mostly of Marimekko wall hangings and Naugahyde beanbag chairs. These were not only comfortable, but also made it comforting to know that I was sitting on a basic food group which could be boiled and eaten in the event that lean years ever returned. I met Ally at one of the many poolside cocktail parties thrown by the building's annoying social director. The first time I saw Ally I knew that she was an interior designer. She had great bedroom eyes. In those superficial days of my youth, I also liked everything else about that first view. Long dark hair, olive skin bronzed by the summer sun (when we still had an ozone layer), the right size, the right look. All parts in apparent working and pert order. But it was those eyes that got me—and I wanted her. It was a

short and classical romantic attack. *Veni, Vidi, Vici,*
although not necessarily in that order. Thirty days after we
met, she moved in with me. Thirty-one days after we met,
she sent all of my furniture to Morgan Memorial. And that
was the beginning of my personal journey of redecoration
that had brought me to the breakfast area in which the
Levin clan was currently gathered.

"So," I said to the assembled family, "ready for a
great new year?"

"I could use a few more months of camp," said
Justin, looking up momentarily from the comic section of
the morning paper.

"Who couldn't?" said Ally. "Today we start the new
Decorators' Show House."

This utterance was so devastating that it caused
Justin to lower the paper midway through Doonesbury,
while I was stuck in a mid-coffee slurp. "Show House!"
These two words struck greater fear into the hearts of Buzz
and Justin than "Niagara Falls" did to Curly, Larry and
Moe. The idea seems simple enough. Each year a charitable
organization, usually the Women's League, takes over a big
old unoccupied home. Designers tour the house and submit
decorating plans for individual rooms. A committee chooses
the winning plans, assigns the designers their rooms, and
coordinates things as the work is done.

Like so many things in life, the telling is simpler
than the doing. The charitable committee is despotic and
the designers are competitive egomaniacs. And when all are
placed together under one roof, frantically working to outdo
each other, the Balkans suddenly seem, by contrast, to be a
relaxing vacation destination. That is, except for my sweet
patootie, of course, whom I now regarded with a diffident
glance.

"I thought you were through with these things," I
said hopefully.

"Darling, I was. But this year the Women's League has taken over this glorious townhouse on Beacon Hill. They made a deal with some rich Middle Eastern financier who bought it from an estate. It's been vacant for years, but it's supposed to be phenomenal." She obviously noted the looks of disquietude on the faces of her husband and son. "Oh come on, guys," she pouted. "This'll be in all the national magazines and it won't take all of my time. I'll still be home to reheat leftovers."

"Doesn't there have to be something first," asked Justin, "in order for it to become a leftover?"

"Mere details," said Ally, waving her napkin in his smiling face. "And that is why I keep your father around, because lawyers are so good with details. Time for school. Time for work. See you boys later."

That said, Ally kissed us both and retreated upstairs. I looked at the clock.

"Let's make tracks, kiddo. The eighth grade awaits."

SOME FREE ADVICE FROM ALLYN

Hand-painted details make any room special. For example, paint roses and vines under the ceiling molding in a bedroom. In a kitchen, trompe l'oeil techniques can be used on cabinets to make them look like chicken coops with painted wire fronts enclosing chickens.

THREE

Justin and I got into my car, which was still covered with the last salt spray from driving through low tides and over dunes, and headed off for school. Ally and I drove Range Rovers. Hers is black, mine white. I anguished over this choice, especially as we were now out of the era of wretched excess and into the age of restraint. But we had become devout Range Rover fans, and loved the car's combination of Anglophile snobbery and urban attack qualities. We also like sitting high above everyone else, knowing that if things got too tough, we could always jump a curb and escape through the fields. If we could ever find any fields.

"I thought she was through with these shows," Justin said, unwilling to drop the last subject.

"What can I say? Decorators are a strange lot. You know the old saying, 'Can't live with them, can't buy a couch without them.'"

"Seems like an awful lot of work to me."

"There are some people who love to be surrounded by the excitement of back-stabbing neurotic competitors. Besides," I added, "your mother's talented and oblivious to her overly competitive peers."

"Yeah," Justin said, "but they call all night long. 'What room did Carolina get?' 'How could Ramon pick those wallpapers?' 'Can you believe that chintz?'"

"Very impressive," I said. "You're getting better at the lingo each year."

"Are you kidding?" Justin said. "Yesterday some guy called and told me to tell Mom he wanted some ideas about tschotchkes."

"Tell him to keep away from your mother's tschotchkes," I said.

"I don't think you'll have to worry about that guy, Dad. But, what's a tschotchke anyway?"

"Why not ask your Latin teacher? He can probably conjugate the word for you. Here we are," I said, as we pulled into the school lot. It did my heart good to see all the preps and prepettes ready for the start of a new season. Justin got out and was lost in a sea of blond hair and blue blazers. This was his second year at private school and I still was not completely acculturated. We were not exactly an old family with deep prep school roots. I was a proud graduate of my hometown high school and assumed that my son would continue in this glorious and free tradition. What I hadn't reckoned with was what had happened to public education.

An aging population had decided that lowering property taxes was more important than lowering the size of classrooms. The PTA was involved more with debating the agenda of the politically correct than in troubling itself with the disappearance of academic standards. After the sixth grade, we said goodbye to the neighborhood schools and went off in search of the local equivalent of the playing fields of Eton. It was a new world for the Levins, but maybe it was a new world all around. I waved in the general direction of where I had last seen my pride and joy and headed off for work.

My office is in downtown Boston, so my route is out 128, down to the Mass. Turnpike, and into town. It's much easier to describe the 8 a.m. rush on the route than it is to actually drive it. The traffic is often bumper to bumper. I could choose the radio or just creep along with the flow while lost in thought. Thoughts came easily today. Living through my own years of school and now almost nine of Justin's had permanently adjusted my circadian rhythms so that Labor Day was emotionally if not technically the beginning of the new year. January first may be the day the calendar changes, but for me the new year always begins with the end of summer when school starts again.

My law school days were at Penn in Philadelphia, but I was a Boston boy at heart. After graduation, I came back home, joined a firm, and began to pursue the cruel mistress of law. I had wanted to be a lawyer ever since the fifth grade when my father brought me *The Story of My Life* by Clarence Darrow. My father, a man whose political development froze in the Great Depression, also brought me the life stories of Eugene Debs, John L. Lewis, Paul Robeson, and Earl Browder. Luckily for me, it was Darrow who made the greatest impression. As things turned out, becoming a socialist hero might have been a poor choice.

Darrow, I later came to realize, had the best of both worlds in the law. He could take on great civil liberty cases like the Scopes monkey trial, and he could fight the death penalty in the Leopold and Loeb case. But he could also charge the Leopolds, Loebs, railroads and others enough money to prove it was possible to do good and make good at the same time. So I gave it my best shot, sometimes with good results. For example, at the height of the school busing crisis in Boston, the Boston City Council hung placards from their windows in City Hall criticizing the federal judge and his integration orders. Despite protests, the Mayor claimed he had no control over the City Council windows. He also said publicly that he "wished there was something he could do." I was able to put his feet to the fire after spending a day in the library and finding an 1810 ordinance that said that any printed matter affixed to City Hall had to be approved by the Mayor. When he refused to respond to my requests, I filed suit and the signs came down. The night I won the case, callers to a radio talk show referred to me as a "Jewish Commie pinko." I had arrived.

This, however, was another year. New dragons to slay. New checks to cash. Thank you, Clarence. Now, if you could just stay in my thoughts and out of my dreams, everything would be terrific.

The radio caught my attention. Imus, a priest, and a rabbi were arguing with Fred about the coming football season. No way to start my new season, I hit the buttons searching for NPR. A series on Dams on the Danube was about to begin. Why the Republicans wanted to kill this show was beyond me. Maybe they recorded these things and played them backwards looking for messages from the Devil. As for me, I was reaching for the button to head back to Imus when the phone rang.

I'm sure the world was a better place without cell phones, which were, with the exception of black and white movie colorization, the curses of the modern world. Long ago, I gave up any hope that my home would be my castle, and when the blue-toothed Blackberry arrived, I realized my automotive fortress of solitude was gone, too. The ringing was like Joshua blowing his trumpet. I turned down the radio as my walls came tumbling down. "Good morning, dahling," I said.

"Oh Buzz," she said, "you knew it was me. How sweet."

"I am sweet, yes, which has nothing to do with the fact that your number showed up. And besides, who else would call? Anyway, enough about me, what's up with you?"

"Well," she sighed, "after spending all that time together on vacation, I miss you already."

"Do you want to talk dirty to me on the phone?"

"Absolutely," she replied, "as soon as you tell me where my keys are."

"I knew there was a catch. Have you looked in the drawer next to the back door where you put them so you wouldn't forget them?" The phone went dead and in a moment she was back. "See. I still need you. Well, I'm off for a big day on Beacon Hill."

"Are you sure you wouldn't rather stay home and spend your time de-balling sweaters, like other wives?"

"It's a thought," she responded, "but women cannot live by de-balling alone."

"Tell that to some of my male divorce clients."

"I'm going underground, Allyn. So listen, good luck—call me later." I nosed the car into the narrow drive that led to the underground parking lot and slowed at the guard booth.

"Good morning, Mr. Levin," yelled the fellow who ran the garage and whose name continued to elude me. "Did you have a nice summer?"

"Terrific," I yelled, all the while remembering the old line, "what was, was." I pulled into my space and the start of a new season, ready to see what would be.

FOUR

I got out of the car and decided to start the year off right by taking the stairs instead of the elevator. My office was on the twenty-second floor, and I jogged up the one flight of stairs that connected the garage to the lobby. That was about enough, so I headed for the elevator, slightly winded and not at all exhilarated. Getting back to my regular routine, I picked up the *Boston Herald* from the newsstand. The *Herald* is a quasi-tabloid with aspirations. As a result, I could usually get a good summary of the previous day's news, gossip, and sex crimes by the time the elevator reached my floor.

I got off the elevator and looked to the right. Good news—we were still in business. I could see through the glass doors to the conference room and out the window to the expanse of ocean. These were the offices of Shapiro, Martin, Sartore and Levin. Not exactly one of Boston's oldest legal establishments, but certainly one with a terrific view of the harbor and Logan Airport. A good place to practice law, a great place to daydream. So far so good; my partners had not removed my name from the door and the receptionist still recognized me. Everything seemed to be in its place.

I looked down the hall into Sam Martin's office. He was busy tapping golf balls into an overturned coffee cup. Martin did estate planning and the administration of estates. The bulk of his practice centered on hanging around with rich people, and a firm stroke was essential. I waved and he shook his putter back at me.

"Hiya, boss," said my secretary, looking ready for business. Her long, two-toned fingernails were poised for their first typing assignment of the new year. Her hair was newly coifed, tress upon tress hanging to her shoulders. A nice miniskirt, far better than average legs, and incredibly spiked heels.

"Lisa, you're still working. I was sure this was going to be sugar daddy summer."

"I wish. I keep falling for great bodies with no bankrolls. I'm almost twenty-seven. My economic clock keeps ticking. How many more years do you think I've got before wealthy elderly men find me too old?"

I was speechless. "Your mail and messages are on your chair," she continued.

"What's in store for me this morning?"

"You've got Mrs. Hirsch in about three minutes about her divorce, Bean called twice because he's nervous about his trial, and the partners want to meet."

"Who sent us this Mrs. Hirsch?"

"She said she's a friend of Gail Miller. Remember? You represented her when she got divorced from her husband, Malcolm."

I smiled at Lisa. "This could be big. It's not every day we start off with a referral from Malcolm's ex."

Lisa looked at me, her expression unchanged. "Should I make a note of that in the file?"

"It was just a joke, Lisa." Now she showed signs of a pout in formation. "I think I'll go into my office," I said. "Keep in touch."

I entered, sat down, put my feet up and looked out

over the harbor. Strange to say, but I was happy to be back. I loved the law and spent so much time at it that this room was like home. Naturally, my live-in decorator had been responsible for my legal inner space. I sat behind a mahogany early nineteenth-century partner's desk facing two wing chairs. There was a long custom-designed credenza behind my chair into which I stuffed most of my papers to give the room an illusion of neatness. Ally had put up faux marbleized crown molding, a beige rug and textured beige wallpaper, the only detail about which I had been consulted were the antique maps on the walls.

Actually, the maps were part of a collection I was building. History had always been my favorite subject in school and vestiges of intellectual curiosity remained even these many years later. Maps from the seventeenth and eighteenth centuries were hand-colored and fanciful, combining both art and an interesting view of the world. I had managed to acquire Speed's map of the Northeast, done in 1676. The English had seized New Amsterdam from the Dutch in 1664 and Speed made the first map to use the words "New York." Niue Holland had disappeared from earlier charts and in its place for the first time appeared Cape Cod. Across from my desk was a British field map from the revolutionary war that showed rebel gun placements around Boston Harbor. These maps and various tidal and shipping lane charts from the colonial era all hung in the spots most attorneys reserved for their diplomas and pictures of themselves shaking hands with famous politicians or golfers. When I needed something more current and personal than the Belgian Leo to look at, I could swivel my chair to look at the photos of Justin and me traversing the China Bowl at Vail. These were shot in the rare moments when I was upright.

Ally was also responsible for decorating the rest of the firm's offices. She did this in a style that could be called English Library. Rich colors and classic furniture gave the impression of a long and stately history. In truth, the other names on the door and I were of more recent vintage. We had all once been employed by one of Boston's larger traditional outfits. But we hated taking orders from people we thought were less competent, objected to having to account for our time to an office manager, and ultimately thought we could have more fun on our own, and even make more money, so we gave it a try.

We set up shop and have never had any regrets. Martin, the aforementioned golfer, ministers to the needs of the dead and near dead. Shapiro concentrates on the necessities of corporations with their attendant wheeler dealers. Sartore and I spend our time litigating, defending, or prosecuting, depending upon which client needs what. Over the years we've managed to add a few associates and paralegals. We are growing old together, but still think of ourselves as brash-though-polished kids, regularly beating the crap out of the old Boston crowd.

The intercom buzzed and Lisa announced the arrival of Mrs. Hirsch. I asked Lisa to bring her and some coffee in. I knew a little about the Hirsches. They were very rich and very glitzy. No charitable event or opening would be complete without their donation and their chauffeured Rolls-Royce arrival. Boston is not L.A., and a Rolls still turns heads on this coast.

Mrs. Hirsch walked in the door, and I could see that she, too, had the ability to turn heads. Not many women come to see a lawyer at 10 a.m. wearing an outfit that can best be described as hooker chic. I knew nothing about her cash assets, but her open blouse and obscenely short skirt left little doubt about her more tangible ones. I looked forward to her sitting down. Things were definitely looking up.

"Please sit down, Mrs. Hirsch," I offered, not knowing whether I should stand or sit, a question not of manners but of view.

"Call me Karen."

"Call me Buzz."

"Let's get to the point," she began. "I married garbage, I lived with garbage, and God help me, I even ate garbage. Now I want you to take out the garbage."

How sweet. I looked again at the woman across the table. It was time to refocus, this time on the face. Hers was pleasant enough, but if the eyes are the windows to the soul, a vacancy sign should have been hanging from her nose. This was no beautiful nymph arrived to charm me back to autumn work but, alas, a first class bimbo. So, I began the task of finding out what the case was all about.

The Hirsches were currently living in an estate in the very posh suburb of Weston. Mr. Hirsch—Bill to his friends—had humbler origins. He had begun his working career in Chelsea as a scrap dealer in metal and rubber. His flat feet had kept him home from the Vietnam War and, while home, his scrap dealings around the world made him rich. He started buying companies. One, a small manufacturer of condoms, had recently made him even richer. According to Mrs. Hirsch, her husband was wont, as she so delicately put it, "to fuck everything that moved." As a result, he was in the forefront of the movement to safe sex.

Based upon personal use and experience, in the mid '80s, he'd seen that rubbers were the way of the future. Through clever advertising, colorizing, and even NBA player endorsements, he made sure that his were the rubbers of choice. Known far and wide as the King of Condoms, he was even heard to remark that AIDS had been very good to him.

To Karen, a high school dropout who'd met her husband while working as a perfume promotional salesgirl (better known as a "spritzer") at Filene's, the cars, furs, and homes more than made up for the jerk to whom she was married. But recently there'd been some problems. It seems that, like their maker, Hirsch's products were less than perfect. This was demonstrated when a very pregnant young woman showed up at their door to announce that she was about to have Bill's baby. This in itself was no catastrophe that money couldn't handle until Bill announced that he and what's-her-name were moving in together. He was in love and ready to start a new family. And so saying, he packed his bags, hollered for the chauffeur, and off they'd gone.

My fascination with Karen's tolerance increased when she told me that she was still unperturbed by these events. The future without Bill was not a devastating thought. However, the next day, when she decided to do some therapeutic shopping and discovered that her house charge at Cartier had been closed and that the American Express Black Card was shut down, she'd had enough.

"So, I wanna clean the shithead out," she ended.

"It's why my father worked long hours to send me to Yale," I responded with a pleasant smile that drew only a "Huh?"

"Rest easy, Karen," I said as I ushered her to the door. "I'll hire detectives. We'll tie him up in attachments and restraining orders. I'll march through his documents like Sherman on the way to the sea."

"Is that Murray Sherman?" she asked. "Because if it is, we once had a little thing, and I'd just as soon he didn't know what's happening."

This was no Jeopardy fan, I thought. "Don't you worry. Murray won't know a thing. Just go home and wait for my call. In the meantime, you can help by going through all of your husband's papers. Look through files, envelopes, folders."

"What am I looking for? I don't know much about business."

That was undoubtedly her first foray into understatement. I tried to make it easy. "Look for numbers and dollar signs."

She stood up, smoothing her diminutive skirt. "Brilliant," she said, as she did me the favor of leaning over to pick up her purse, an accessory for which several alligators had given their lives. "I knew you were a great lawyer."

As I ushered her to the door, I thought there was something unnervingly familiar about those last lines. She left and the intercom sounded.

"Your wife on line three."

I pushed the button, and was about to say hello, when Allyn yelled through the phone, "Get over here right away—somebody tried to kill Megan."

"That's terrible," I said. "Who would want to kill her?"

"Most of the people who know her," Ally replied. Shock had not dimmed her senses.

"Good point. Okay, so it's not so terrible. Which brings me to the next point. Why do you want me to come over?"

"Someone bashed her head in with a hammer or something. The police say we're all suspects and you're my alibi. Besides, the place is full of police and there's an ambulance, so shouldn't there be a lawyer?"

"I'm on the way. Don't let anyone who looks like they can afford me confess until I get there."

SOME DESIGN TIPS

Bathroom sink cabinets are much more comfortable if the tops are thirty-six inches from the floor. Box springs should be built up four inches on legs. Decorators always upholster the box springs and legs, even if they are under the dust ruffle.

FIVE

Yelling "Take messages, I'll be back," I rushed out the door and into the elevator. Exiting the building, I decided that I could make better time on foot than by car, so I briskly walked toward Beacon Hill. Crimes and their criminals usually come to me long after the event, often at bail hearings or arraignments, so it was with some excitement that I walked up the hill to the scene of the crime.

My spirits were somewhat altered by my acquaintance with the victim. I knew enough about Megan to have already started drawing up a list of suspects that included her ex-husband and most of her ex-clients. At the State House, I started to puff a bit.

Colonial Boston originally had three hills. Luckily for me, only Beacon Hill still survives, the other two had been leveled and Beacon Hill lowered as the Back Bay and the Harbor were filled in to accommodate a growing population and businesses. There's a plaque hanging on a wall next to my office building that indicates where the British landed their ships after being spied by Paul Revere. It's a pretty good walk from that colonial dock to the current waterfront. It was also a pretty good walk from my office to

Beacon Hill, but at least after the State House the walk turned downhill.

Beacon Hill had always been, in real estate brokers' parlance, Boston's most desirable neighborhood. Its twisting narrow streets held the brick and brownstone homes built in the nineteenth century for captains of the ocean and the industrial revolution. Like most of Boston, a street map of the area defied logic, as cart paths had turned into circles and squares of homes. Show House, an annual charity event run by the Boston Women's League, was in a Louisburg Square brownstone. Once the enclave of Cabots, Lowells, and other Brahmins of note, now anyone with the price of admission—six to twelve million dollars, depending on the house—would be admitted. A Lodge and a Litvak could now easily be next-door neighbors and, were it not for the police cars that converged this morning, anyone passing by would think that caste and cash were living happily ever after.

Louisburg Square was usually a safe haven for the Women's Leaguers, most of whom could have been cast as extras in *The Late George Appley*. But today, the milling boys in blue made a beautiful addition to the flowered skirts in pink and green. As I got closer, similarities between the Leaguers and the cops began to appear. In addition to uniforms, both groups were wearing sensible shoes and name badges. I was willing to bet that if the cops loosened their ties, they would all reveal gold chains, which, although not having been passed down for three generations, served the same purpose as the simple pearls that adorned the elegant necks of the group that stood before me.

I walked through the crowd and up the stairs, fighting back the urge to yell out "Oh, Muffy" to see how many responded. This was some house. The entryway itself was large enough for two units of low-income housing. I walked around and saw a dining room that could be used for Boston Celtics scrimmages. Whoever owned this place was way beyond comfortable. There were groups of people in the living room. Ally was in there, talking to a tall, young policeman who was hovering over her, either hanging on her every word or trying to look down her blouse. She needed her lawyer.

She saw me coming and waved me over. She introduced me to her new friend, who went off to question witnesses.

"So what gives?" I asked.

"Unbelievable," she said. "There was an opening meeting in the dining room. All of the decorators were there except for Megan and Bruno. There was some idle chatter about how we might find them in the bedroom together. Rumors have been circulating that they were becoming business partners and were spending an inordinate amount of time together. Anyway, we started to tour the house. We went from the dining room into the living room. Really a beautiful space—I could do a nice English look in there—"

"The attack," I reminded her.

"Right. So, we finish the living room and enter the butler's pantry on the way to the kitchen. What a pantry. You've heard of 'to die for'? Well, this place is to live for. Beautiful inlaid panels on huge doors. Anyway, someone, maybe Melissa, opens one of the doors and out falls a body. You can imagine the scene. Melissa screams, Frankie screams, we all scream. But we weren't loud enough to wake the dead, which is what we thought we were looking at. A couple of the guys get up the nerve to stretch out the body, because we didn't know who it was. Well, it was Megan, except that her head was partially wrapped up in some fabric that was all covered with dried blood. I'm the only lawyer's wife, so I yell, 'Don't touch anything!' Someone cries out that he'll call the police.

"Let me tell you," she continued. "My guess is that it was really tough for some of the people not to touch anything."

"To see if she was alive?" I asked.

"No, to check the labels. There was serious knock-off speculation."

"That's what these people think about," I said, looking around. "It was her head that was knocked off, not her outfit."

"You know, Buzz, she isn't well liked. She isn't even liked. But anyway, back to the story. While we were waiting for someone to call the police, Johnny Bishop—you know, Bishop's of Boston?—decides to ignore my advice and feels Megan's neck. He yells out, 'There's a pulse, she's still alive,' and he rips off the fabric and starts giving her mouth-to-mouth. The EMTs come running in, congratulate Johnny for saving her life, and rush her off on a stretcher. So here we are."

I looked around the room and spotted a lieutenant who appeared to be in charge. I recognized him from some previous cases and walked over to get some information. Here was another case of a character from central casting. Anyone who has read *Make Way for Ducklings* would mistake him for Officer O'Malley's older brother. Not only did he have the map of Ireland all over his face, he had it all over his necktie. Literally. It was the strangest cravat I had ever seen. This man should never have been let out of uniform. It did, however, go with the rumpled tweed blazer. Maybe it was time the police had a detective dress code. Maybe they did and this was it.

"Hello, counselor. Aren't you supposed to wait until I arrest someone before you show up?"

"Ally, you remember Lieutenant Daley. He's busted some of my finest clients."

"A pleasure, Mrs. Levin," said the Lieutenant. "I take it you were here working on the Show House."

"She was," I replied. "So what gives?"

"Well," he said, "according to the forensics boys who know about dried blood and the like, it seems that around midnight last night someone attacked the victim with a blunt instrument, inflicting sufficient blows to the head to render her unconscious, probably comatose. She had some cloth wrapped around her head, which leads us to believe that the assailant snuck up on her, threw the cloth over her head, and brained her. Whoever did it probably figured she was dead. It was quite a smash on the noggin."

"She wasn't supposed to be here last night," said Allyn. "The house was closed and none of the decorators were allowed in."

The Lieutenant told us that Megan had been stuffed in a closet along with her belongings, which included a tape measure and note pad. "It appears that she was trying to get a jump on the competition. Maybe some of the competition got a jump on her," added Daley. "How important is this Show House?"

"When the House is finished, thirty thousand people walk through it. It's the best advertising and exposure a Boston decorator can get and leads to a lot of work," explained Allyn. "Megan had been out of Show House for a couple of years and had told people she was coming back in this year to make a big splash. Something we'd all remember."

"I doubt that this is what she had in mind," I added.

My remark went unnoticed as the young policeman came up rather hurriedly to our group. "Lieutenant," he said, "you've got to go up to the fourth floor. Quickly. There's another one."

"Holy shit," Daley said. "Look—you stay at the front door and put Brownfield around back. No one gets out."

"You two come with me," he said and, thus drafted, my wife and I ran up the stairs behind him.

The trouble I'd had walking up Beacon Hill was nothing compared to the dash up four flights. Like many of the old townhouses, the top floor had originally been meant as living quarters for the help. As a result, the staircase between the third and fourth floor became narrow and steep, and we ran up in close single file, with me bringing up the rear. Fortunately for me, Ally was in the middle, so the rear I brought up and kept bumping into was her familiar Armani-clad derriere. Only the cloud cast by the thought of "murder most foul" was able to banish other lewd and lascivious thoughts that would have naturally occurred in my current position.

We reached the fourth floor and I had to struggle to catch my breath. I was relatively certain that, of all the people in the house, I was only in better shape than Megan.

We arrived at a narrow hall that had several rooms off of it. The sound of dripping water caught our attention and we followed it to the end of the hall. An unhappy looking policeman was standing at the door and blocked our way after the lieutenant entered.

In a moment, Daley came out of the room.

"I don't know how strong your stomachs are, but I could use an identification," he said to us. Ally and I exchanged glances, shrugged and entered the room.

What immediately caught my attention were the contrasting colors. The body sitting up in the half-filled tub wore a bright yellow suit that I remembered seeing in a Versace menswear advertisement. I always wondered who would wear a suit like that. But the yellow of the suit was muted compared to the bright purple of the face that stood out from the collar. The face's eyes were bugged out and a cord was wrapped tightly around the neck. I turned away and looked at Ally, who had turned as white as the tile in the room. I fought back a tide of bile rising in my throat. Ally looked like she was in the midst of the same struggle as she bent over with her hand covering her mouth.

We recovered. The body in the tub did not.

"You guys okay?" Daley asked. We both agreed that we would survive.

Daley walked over and felt the deceased's wrist.

"Looking for a pulse?" I ventured.

"Not likely," said Daley. "If the suit is a clue, then this may have been a very limp wrist in life. In death, it's still not too stiff. Rigor mortis hasn't had time to set in yet. My guess is this one was killed earlier today, hours after Megan got knocked out. By the way, what's his name?"

"Bruno," said Allyn, looking over at the body. "He's a decorator. Or, I guess, he was. Very successful, high society. Offices in Boston and Palm Beach."

Daley asked if there was a next of kin.

"Sort of," said Ally. "He lived with his partner, Barry. Bruno and Barry. Although I think they had some sort of lover-decorator quarrel. I heard they split up."

"And?" said Daley, looking square into Ally's baby browns.

"And what?" she asked, breaking his gaze to memorize the floor.

"I've questioned enough witnesses to know that you were about to add something, thought better of it, and clammed up."

"Clammed up?" I said. "What is this, *The Maltese Falcon?*"

"He's right, Buzz. There were all these rumors that Bruno had dumped Barry and was joining forces with Megan. I just didn't see any point of dragging Barry into this. He's such a dear."

"'Join forces' is an understatement. They may be redesigning the Pearly Gates if she doesn't recover. When was the last time you saw Barry?" Daley asked.

"He was downstairs with all the other decorators. I think I saw him in the butler's pantry."

Daley turned toward one of the policemen standing nearby. "Roberts, go downstairs and get me the coroner and a decorator named Barry."

While Daley was giving orders, I noticed that Ally had wandered over in the direction of Bruno.

"You know," said Ally, "that isn't just a rope around his neck. It's tassel cording, used to tie back draperies."

"What do you think, Daley?" I said. "Fabric around Megan, tassels strangling Bruno—I wouldn't be surprised to find someone upholstered to death on the second floor."

"Not funny," he added. "But I suppose there is a connection. Who'd want to kill decorators?"

"The word 'client' springs immediately to mind," I suggested.

"Makes you wonder why there are any lawyers left alive," he answered, with a roguish twinkle in otherwise weary eyes.

The policeman named Roberts walked in with the coroner and looked toward Daley. "Nobody's seen Barry since the butler's pantry."

"Well," said Daley, "I doubt the butler did it. Let's go downstairs and see if we can find Barry and some suspects."

"Not to mention breath mints," said Ally.

SIX

Ally and I made our way down the stairs and
through the confusion in the living room.
Policemen were busy taking statements. The news about
Bruno spread quickly and could be traced by the gasps that
traveled around the room. I observed that the only thing
missing from the tableau was someone who needed
comforting. There were no grieving widows or sobbing
relations. Frankly, there may have been quiet elation with
the removal of formidable competition. Megan's next of kin
was a sister from Baltimore; however, they apparently
hadn't spoken in years, and with Megan still alive, I
doubted she was heading north. As for Bruno's formerly
nearest and dearest Barry, he seemed to have vanished.
This observation was not lost on the crowd, and murmurs of
"Where's Barry?" cut through the group.

I looked around at the assembled crowd. Many of
them were familiar from years of accompanying my wife to
her business and business-related social functions. Cheap
jokes aside, it was hard to generalize. Some I knew to be
truly talented. Their finished products actually deserved
the label of "to die for." Others were strictly to die from,
sharing the sense of color and style normally on display in
the lobby of a Holiday Inn. It had just occurred to me how

apt the metaphors of to die for or from were to the day's proceedings, when Ally gently nudged me.

"This has been one hell of a morning," she said, "I think I'll go home and lie down for a while. I can only get so much mileage out of black humor. This is starting to sink in and when it sinks all the way, I won't be able to avoid reality any longer. What about you?"

"Back to work. Another new client is supposed to be in, and then I'm scheduled to talk business with the boys."

"So who do you think did it?"

"If this were the movies, we'd have to find a link between Megan and Bruno, see who was mixed up in the link and find our felon. Barry is probably suspect numero uno. But it isn't the movies, and it's rarely that simple. I've got no ideas, no suspects and I'm late." We walked outside to Ally's car, which was parked right in front of the brownstone. "Great space," I said. There were two dead bodies a hundred yards away, but life had to go on and a parking space on Beacon Hill was one of life's treats.

"Sure you'll be okay?" I asked Ally as I opened the door for her.

"Sure," she said with a half-smile, climbing in and closing the door. "See you later. Maybe we'll have dinner."

Now there's a novel way to end the day, I thought, as I turned and began to walk back up Beacon Hill. What a way to start the new season. All this walking, not to mention murder and mayhem. There was nothing I could do about the crimes, but I saw a taxi, which provided immediate relief to the walking problem.

It was one o'clock in the afternoon when I got back to the office. Lisa was at lunch. I couldn't find the appointment book, but I did remember some kind of meeting was scheduled with a new client. I went into my office, closed the door, and awaited more of the unknown. If only I had been a boxing champion at Princeton, I could ring up Lady Ashley and spend the afternoon drinking absinthe and speaking in short declarative sentences. As it was, my life was much more Perry Mason than Papa Hemingway, so I expectantly got out my yellow legal pad as there was a knock on the door.

I recognized Gina Williams as soon as she walked into the room. She was an anchorwoman on a major network's *Morning U.S.A.* show. I was one of her loyal fans—why not? She was gorgeous. She was brilliant. In her early thirties, slim, blond—she was American apple pie on great legs. A double-gold-medal winner for Best Body on the Beach and Best Mind in the Library. I felt blessed.

Some of my favorite bathroom reading was *Women's Wear Daily.* If memory served me right, Gina was wearing a "simply smashing" Gianfranco Ferré tailored jacket and fantastically short skirt, revealing legs that could have launched more ships than any smile from Helen of Troy. I wondered if she would think ill of me if I began dropping pencils when she sat down.

These thoughts ended when I noticed that Ms. Williams was not alone. The man with her looked rather like a weasel wearing pinstripes. A lawyer, obviously. As Gina sat, I sensed the enigmatic juxtaposition of desire and boredom, suspecting, however, that it was my desire and her boredom. The weasel approached.

"Mr. Levin, my name is M. Louis Brecher. I'm Ms. Williams' lawyer."

I couldn't believe it—an unctuous New York accent. What was she doing with the likes of him? On the other hand, what was she doing with the likes of me?

The answer followed. "We've been referred to you regarding a lawsuit that has been brought against Ms. Williams. It's an unusual case. Frankly, we've heard that you have a reputation for handling cases that are unusual and have high visibility. What we have is very delicate and personal."

"What we have, Louis, is a load of crap," Gina said. I'd never heard the words "load of crap" spoken more beautifully. Two beautifully full lips enunciating the "p" to perfection. "Look, Mr. Levin," she continued.

"Buzz."

"Okay, Buzz. I've been sued by my former husband, the esteemed professor Harold Goodman, of Harvard Law School."

"I never knew you were married to him," I said. Harold Goodman was, as he would tell you himself, a brilliant scholar. He would probably add "world's greatest legal mind." He was a famous mastermind in the defense of the indefensible. He was a fixture at both the Supreme Court and Oprah, where he was quick to tell Justice and talk show host alike how they should be thinking on any number of subjects.

"The whole marriage lasted a few miserable months. When I discovered that all he wanted from me was a ticket to social acceptance and that he could never love anyone but himself, I called it quits. The good news is that I had a child. The bad news is that he's the father. We were divorced and he was ordered to pay child support. He told off the judge, was held in contempt, and now appears to be obsessed with revenge. This suit is the first shot."

She handed me a package of legal documents. On first reading, it seemed that Professor Goodman had come up with a novel legal theory. In his suit, he claimed that she seduced him, got herself pregnant and threatened him into marriage. He alleged that when she was ready to give birth she threw him out, filed for divorce and got child support. His conclusion was that the whole thing was a scheme to trick him into first contributing his superior genes to her future child and then his money to support the little genius.

I looked up from the papers.

"What do you think?" she asked.

"'A noble mind here overthrown,' in my humble

opinion. Talk about making new law. First there was alimony, then palimony, now this guy has invented stud-imony."

"Oh God," she muttered. "What a headline for the *Enquirer*. What are we going to do? The publicity will be miserable. You know how tough it is for a woman in this business."

Call me politically incorrect, but I couldn't imagine that anything was or ever would be tough for Gina Williams. "What I'm going to do, Gina," I said, using her first name as I warmed for the battle, "is file enough papers to show Goodman that if he doesn't drop the case, I'll turn *him* into such a public fool he won't even be able to get a spot on *Letterman*, let alone be taken seriously by any law student again. He either caves in or checks out."

The intercom rang and I picked it up. "Excuse me a minute. Yes, Lisa."

"Your wife on line one, boss. I think it's another emergency."

I pressed the line.

"Buzz. You've got to do something. They just arrested Barry. He wants you to be his lawyer. I've got to hang up—this is all too incredible to deal with a moment longer." And hang up she did.

I knew that the call was a command performance. I would have loved to have spent more time talking tough to impress Gina and make Brecher feel incompetent, but it was not to be.

"Gina, Louis," I said, "there's been a bit of an emergency, but don't worry, I'll start filing papers tomorrow. I'll march through him like Sherman on the way to the sea." I halted expectantly, but the only response was a warm smile and a brief kiss on the cheek.

"Thank you, Buzz," she said, never once mentioning Murray Sherman, as I had known she wouldn't. My head was light. My knees were wobbly. I almost forgot to ask for a retainer. But not quite.

DON'T FORGET

Never call curtains "draperies" or "drapes"—this is very déclassé and never done by people in the know.

SEVEN

My partners and associates had all assembled in the conference room. When *Boston Legal* became a popular television series, Sartore had convinced us that we should have meetings just like a TV law firm. I was happier with older shows like *Miami Vice* that inspired us to just meet for drinks. Even *Ally McBeal* would have been a welcome change. But Jack's television tastes were stuck in more formal legal shows and he insisted on real meetings, and so reality TV it was.

I knew what awaited me. My designing wife had procured "just the right" brass inlaid mahogany conference table that could seat about twenty. The room had sailing and whaling prints on the walls, a built-in bar and a silver samovar. We kept trying to move in video screens and a blackboard but she had banished them to a back interior conference room. Utility had no place in her finest schemes. My partners would be spread out around the room. Each of them would have an agenda in front of him, prepared by Sartore in various fonts and underlinings. Knights of the Rectangle Table, we called ourselves. They hated these meetings as much as I did, but they were stuck.

Actually, "stuck" was a mild description. A quagmire of bureaucracy and nitpicking drivel was what usually surrounded us. We were a group who spent years learning the law and refining our skills. Clients from around the world sought us out. Yet, looking down at the neatly placed pages on the table, it appeared that today we would be discussing issues which included whether or not to change the coffee selection to French Roast and the financial implications of too much rug shampooing. I was sorry for Barry, but his arrest could not have come at a better time.

"Levin, you're late," said Sartore as I opened the door. He was looking at the Mickey Mouse pocket watch we had given him last year.

"Stuff it, old bean," I replied, "There's murder in the air, the game is afoot, and I'm off." I found the Sherlock-Shakespeare combo exeunt to be most effective at times like this. By the time the listener figures out what you're talking about, you're out the door.

And, so saying, I headed for the elevator. As I was walking out, I could hear Shapiro saying that since he had no intention of discussing recycling office waste paper without all the partners, he was leaving. Sartore was pleading with them to stay. Only someone who had never attended a partner's meeting would think me too callous to consider these crimes a lucky break.

Actually, I was excited by the prospect of a new murder client. Hirsch and Williams would pay the bills, but they weren't the grist for the mill of great law. Defending the accused, that was the stuff. And if the accused happened to be an underdog it was even better. Well, the game may have been afoot, but I had walked enough for one day. I retrieved my faithful Rover from the garage and headed off for the Boston Municipal Court—BMC for short. The legal/financial center of Boston was relatively compact, and I was able to shoot up State Street, park in Center Plaza, and make it to the Court House in fifteen minutes. If I remembered Barry correctly from the few social events at which we had met, these would be fifteen minutes too many.

Barry was waiting for me in one of the holding cells. There were actually two cells. Barry was in one, the other held an assemblage of Hell's Angel wannabes and drunken Nazi pseudo-surfers. Barry cut an amazing contrast as he sat quietly in a white linen suit, pale yellow shirt, and white tie, looking much like a montage of *Tom Wolfe sits in for Oscar Wilde at Reading Gaol.*

"I thought I better put him by himself or the next letter I got would be from some pinko at the ACLU," said the guard, an enlightened civil servant who, except for the badge, appeared indistinguishable from the human refuse in the adjoining cell. (Of course, had they been my clients I would probably refer to them as political prisoners of an unjust system. But, thankfully, they weren't and they could remain detritus until their court-appointed lawyer showed up.)

"How thoughtful," I said. "Those sensitivity courses must be working." I motioned Barry over. He stood up, meticulously wiping the dirt of former cell sitters from his suit.

"Oh, Buzz," he whispered, "thanks for coming. You've got to get me out of here. I simply can't spend another moment next to those people." He motioned to the other incarcerees, who greeted this gesture with hoots and whistles.

"Look," I said, "I'll see you next door for the end of the day arraignments. We'll talk. You'll make bail. We'll talk some more."

I went around the corner and entered the First Session of the Boston Municipal Court. It was to this room that the police brought their most recent arrests for arraignment and bail. As usual, the room was crowded with a diurnal assortment of hookers, muggers, and small time crooks. In my college sociology classes, I was taught that these victims of anomie had been dealt a cruel hand by society. In my later life, I was becoming more certain that these were victimizers, not victims. But my waxing philosophical would have to wait for another day. The court came to order as the bailiff announced that the judge was about to enter the room.

I stood and looked around. The BMC was in the structure known as the "new" courthouse. This name had stuck since 1939 when it was built as a WPA project. It had probably been built with the best of intentions. It provided a number of jobs during the depression and looked like a court was supposed to look. There was an elevated wooden desk for the judge, known as the bench. Below the bench were the table and chairs for lawyers, surrounded by a wooden railing known as the bar. (Admission to this rarefied spot could be obtained by "passing the bar.") The spectators sat behind the bar on low wooden benches. There was a dock for the accused to stand. The problem with the courthouse was that it was far from new and upkeep seemed to have been disregarded. Cleaning for the last fifty years must have been an occasional broom. It was probably last dusted for the Sacco and Vanzetti arraignment. The windows were broken and didn't open. Dust was as plentiful on the furniture as down on a goose. The whole place was a good reason to avoid being arrested or, for that matter, becoming a lawyer.

The door opened and the Honorable Elijah Adams entered. This would not be considered a boon for us. Judge Adams was the oldest working jurist left in Massachusetts, an "old darling" to Horace Rumpole. He played to the crowd and never gave a sucker or a defendant an even break. Prosecutors were treated like favored children, defense lawyers like despised in-laws. He tolerated no one, and I had a hunch that a gay decorator in a white suit would be as well received as Bin Laden at a Texas barbeque.

The traditional purpose of bail was to make sure that a defendant showed up for trial. It was linked to the concept that a person charged with a crime enjoyed the presumption of innocence until proven guilty. Judge Adams was otherwise inclined, and I was glad that Barry was a successful decorator. It was going to take the profit from a few high-priced armoires to get him out.

"Commonwealth v. Barry Stapleton," intoned the clerk, as Barry was led into the dock. "Mr. Stapleton, you are charged with one count of murder in the first degree and one count of assault and battery with a deadly weapon."

"We'll waive the full reading of the charges, and plead not guilty," I said. "Your Honor, could we have second call on this so that I can speak to the prosecutor about bail?"

"Mr. Levin apparently thinks this is one of those fancy country clubs where you get to pick your own tee-time," said Judge Adams to no one in particular. "Why, of course, counselor. I'll be here all day. Take your time because I can't imagine what good it will do."

"Thank you, Your Honor." Trial law is one of the few professions where obsequiousness can sometimes be a virtue. I nodded to the prosecutor and we walked into the hall.

The prosecutor was named Vivian Bis-something-or-other. She was mousy to a T, dressed in K-Mart regalia, and in serious need of an upper lip and sideburn shave. These, too, were ominous signs. Prosecuting in the BMC was the bottom rung of the ladder for aspiring Assistant District Attorneys. They handled only the preliminary part of a case before it was turned over to a seasoned superior. Therefore, most young assistant D.A.'s believed they could impress their superiors by being tough and unyielding. I have also found, and I say this based on purely statistical evidence, that of all these young toughs, the worst are the unattractive women. Call me a sexist, but my own objective surveys have shown that women prosecutors who never got the call for a prom date are most likely to go for a defendant's balls. I admit that Barry added a tricky wrinkle to this scenario, but the odds favored a predictable outcome of my bail negotiations.

"So tell me, Vivian," I said in my most affable tone, "what is my client alleged to have done?"

"Mr. Levin—"

"Buzz."

"Mr. Levin. The D.A.'s office has developed evidence that will demonstrate that for the last two weeks Mr. Stapleton had been harassing Mrs. Megan O'Connor by telephone, mail, and in person. That the day before the crimes he interrupted a lunch that Ms. O'Connor and his former lover, Bruno Cassiani, were having together and that he was heard threatening to kill them both. And that on the day of the murder he was seen at the Show House coming down the stairs while everyone was crowded around Megan. Last, but by no means least, when officers went to arrest him, he had a rope-like material hanging from his pocket which matched the cord wrapped around Bruno's neck. Shall we go back into court?" She turned and walked briskly back into the courtroom.

It could be worse, I thought. Loads of circumstantial evidence could make a case, but at least there were no eyewitnesses or confessions. She hadn't even mentioned DNA. But I had no time for pondering. If I were late, Judge Adams would probably execute my client and claim harmless error.

The case was called again and the lovely Vivian got up and told the judge exactly what she'd just told me. He looked at me with the same excited demeanor that must have beamed from Madame DeFarge as she awaited the next head.

I rose. "You know as well as anyone, Judge, that the statements of the assistant district attorney are mere allegations. We are not here to determine my client's guilt or innocence—"

"Lucky for him," muttered the judge, loud enough for the room to hear.

"...but to set bail. Barry Stapleton has never been arrested for so much as littering—"

"Looks like he's starting at the top," muttered the man in the black robe.

I met him head-on. "It may look that way only to those who have no background in the constitution or the history of jurisprudence. He stands before you an innocent man. He has lived in this community all of his life. He is well known—"

"Did you say well blown?" asked Judge Adams, sending himself into a fit of laughter.

"Look, Judge, let's save everyone a lot of time. My client can't get a fair shake in this courtroom. Just set bail so that I can appeal, you can be on the front page of the *Boston Globe* again, and public faith in this court can drop another notch."

Sometimes you can win too big. Even Vivian sensed this and, not wanting to lose an appeal or have Judge Adams bounced off the case, she quickly interjected, "Judge, the state would be happy with $20,000 cash bail."

"Are you kidding? $50,000. Not a penny less. You hear me, Levin? Fifty thousand bucks or Barry spends the night picking up soap in the jail house showers."

My patience gone, I rose to speak. But I saw Barry waving at me out of the corner of my eye and went over to him.

"Buzz, let's not make a fuss. Call my assistant and he'll bring over the cash."

"You have fifty thousand dollars in cash at your office?"

"Please. Just call and get me out of here."

"Okay," I said. And much to the judge's dismay, I thanked him for his kind attentiveness and told him that we would make bail within the hour.

And we did.

A NOTE FROM ALLYN

In rooms where the ceilings are low, curtains should be taken up to the ceiling, or just under the molding to give the illusion of greater height.

EIGHT

"God, what a dreadful place," Barry muttered looking across at the front steps of the court.

It was almost five o'clock in the afternoon and we were at a small coffee house across the plaza from the Court House. The place was empty enough for us to go in for a private conversation. We sat down in a corner booth.

"I don't want to rattle you, Barry, but the charges against you are enough to keep you in dreadful places for the next two hundred years, and if Megan dies it will be four hundred. We've got some work to do here. I'll need facts, names, dates—the works. Tomorrow I want you at my office at 10 a.m. to meet with me and my investigator. There'll be a trial in a few months and we've got to get ready."

"Buzz, I'm not guilty," he said, looking down at his folded hands.

I found his choice of words interesting. Most defendants tell me they're innocent. He said "not guilty." I wondered if he was being subtle, or was confused, or had watched too much Court TV. At least he didn't tell me he was one hundred percent innocent.

"I'm pleased to hear you say that," I said. "But unless we get our evidence straight, it won't matter. Look, give me some background. Tell me about Bruno and Megan."

"A cunt and a bitch."

Pure poetry. Pity I didn't know which adjective applied to which victim. "That's a nice start, Barry. Perhaps you could expand on it a bit."

And Barry told me the story of his life.

We sat drinking coffee, and I listened to Barry for the next hour. Perhaps he had a need to justify his lifestyle to me, or maybe he wanted to make sure I was a friend as well as a lawyer. In any event, he started with high school, worked his way through college, the service, and decorating. He told me the story of his brief marriage, fight for sexual identity, exit from the closet, and current lifestyle. I paid the most attention when Bruno entered the picture.

Ten years ago, Barry had been working for one of the larger Boston decorating houses. He had talent, but was content to be someone else's employee. One night, he picked up Bruno at a bar. Bruno was handsome, charming, and articulate. He was also broke and unemployed. Their first night together turned into a week, then a month, then permanent. Bruno did more than just live off Barry—he took control of him. He also became his partner. Though Bruno had no idea how to decorate a room, he apparently knew how to work one. He had internal antennae that could sense the presence of moneyed people. He was able to zero in, gaining their confidence and their decorating. Under Bruno's direction, the team of Bruno and Barry became regulars in high society in Boston and Palm Beach. Barry did all the work and Bruno was in charge of the finances. He set outrageous prices, but the more he charged, the more their work became a highly prized status symbol. Bruno's greatest skill was making friends of clients and clients of friends. They spent weekends and vacations at clients' homes and on their yachts. Bruno prided himself on never reaching for a check.

Barry believed that he needed Bruno—both for love and business. But there was trouble in decorators' paradise. Within the last year, Bruno had started traveling by himself more and more. Without any notice, he would fly off to Florida, New York, or even Maine, telling Barry not to worry, he was off prospecting for more gold. However, none of these trips seemed to lead to jobs. And more recently, Bruno had started coming home at two or three in the morning. Barry never said anything, but he was worried. For one thing, too many of his friends were AIDS victims for him to ignore the risks posed by Bruno's potential breach in their monogamous relationship. Also, he knew he was too dependent on Bruno to lose him. But he had to know the truth, so he did what suspicious marital partners have been doing for centuries: he hired a detective.

Two weeks ago, his private eye had called to announce pay dirt. Barry went to the office of Ace Investigations, where he was shown pictures of Bruno entering a room at the Ritz at twelve o'clock on a Wednesday afternoon and leaving two hours later. In the pictures going in, the door was open and it looked like Bruno was walking into an unoccupied bedroom. For the exit shots, the photographer must have been well positioned and hidden because Bruno, looking very tousled, was shot walking out of the room. You could see into the room, see that it was no longer empty, and actually see the occupant, wearing almost nothing, supine on the unmade bed. And apparently, that's where the shit hit the fan.

Because the nooner on the bed was Megan.

NINE

It was now six o'clock and the coffee shop was closing. It was just as well. I stared at Barry and saw only immense sadness and fear. "Look, Barry," I said. "Let's call it quits for today. Go home, get a good night's sleep, and I'll see you in the morning." He nodded and we walked out and down to the street. I decided I couldn't leave without asking the obvious. "I thought he was gay."

"I knew he was gay," said Barry. A taxi spotted us and pulled over and Barry climbed in. "I have no idea what's happening," he said as he lugubriously slouched into the cab and drove off.

I found my car and headed home. What a way to start back after vacation. It had everything—bimbos, bodies, buggery and bail. If this were an episode of *Sesame Street*, today would have been brought to me by the letter B. I was really beat, and I wanted a bottle of bourbon. And a broad. I loved witty self-repartee, especially while driving. I was becoming positively auto-neurotic. I reached my driveway and turned in.

From the outside, the house looked like Ozzie and Harriet slept there. It was white with black shutters. There was no picket fence, but the English garden was an all-American touch. I went in, feeling not like Ozzie but more like Charlie Brown. Every year, Lucy holds the football for him to kick. He knows she's going to pull it away, but he tries anyway, hoping this time will be different.

So, too, night after night, I expectantly walk through the back door and into the kitchen. As always, Maria has set the "eating island" for dinner, complete with a pitcher of ice water. But something is always missing. It's not just that Rick and Dave never come bounding down the stairs to greet their father, or that Harriet's not there in her apron. What's always missing is food: the smell of food, the sense of food, the hint of food. "Food, glorious food."

At least there was vodka in the freezer. I poured myself about eight fingers and yelled out to anyone who cared, "I'm home!"

"We're upstairs!" yelled Allyn. "What did you bring for dinner?"

"I'm the breadwinner, not the bread bringer," I shouted back. "Feed me." I sat down petulantly and started drinking. This was a test of wills and I was going to win. Vodka had at least two major food groups, potatoes and alcohol. Allyn didn't drink and Justin was just a kid. I did drink and I was a grownup. I could outlast them. This year was going to be different.

Finally, Allyn came into the kitchen. "Oh Buzz, I had such a miserable day. Looking at a dead body, listening to gossip at the Show House, trying to find a parking space on Beacon Hill. You can imagine I was in no mood to defrost, let alone heat." Wrapped tightly in a cashmere robe, hair pulled back under a designer baseball cap, she sounded a bit more pathetic than she looked. My hunch was that she was doing her best to hide her anxiety behind luxury accessories and bravado. I looked at her, then down at my drink, and again at her. Even if she were only faux vulnerable, instead of what I expected was the real thing, I sensed a real opportunity here. Until I heard Justin yelling that he was starving.

Who better than a lawyer should know there is no justice? I had lost. With no appeal.

I heard a car door open and looked out to the driveway. A taxi had pulled in and the driver was walking my way carrying two bags, much beloved and well known in the Levin manse.

"What goes better with murder and mayhem than General Gao and ribs," said Allyn. "Pay the man. Let's eat."

"Oh Ally, you're still my sweet patootie. Does this mean I get to bathe you in duck sauce?"

"Only if I get to squeeze the duck," she said with a wink. Wondering what that meant, and whether it entailed pleasure or pain, I assembled my family for the evening meal.

I was immediately suspicious of Maria, who was removing the takeout food from its containers and putting it in bowls before bringing them to the table.

"She must want something," I whispered to Ally. "What's she up to?"

"She said something before about you signing some papers for her."

"Immigration?"

"No," said Ally. "I think she mentioned Bloomingdale's."

"I'm starved," said Justin as he entered the kitchen and took his usual place. We were all grouped around the eating island. Much of the progress of American home life could be tied directly to the interplay of technology and interior design. Early man ate, slept, cooked—did everything in one room. Technology consisted of fire. Interior design was a few cave drawings. There wasn't much of a living to be made from scratching the occasional bison on a wall, and for designers those were the dark ages. Things picked up a bit as early hovels developed into homes, and the ancients decided that life would be improved by having different rooms for eating, sleeping, sitting and cooking. History does not record this great beginning, and no one then could have known that these simple living arrangements were to be the dawn of decorating. Whether it began in Ur or Chaldea, the records are silent. However, interior decorators flourished in ancient Greece, where they were well paid and assumed special positions.

As science marched forward, so did the decorators. The invention of sliding glass doors, butcher block, granite, marble, and Corian were as big to this industry as unlocking the secrets of the atom to others. There could now be three areas in which to eat: there was the standard dining room, decorated formally and only used for special events; the breakfast room, decorated informally, usually leading out to the garden and yard, and often used for regular family meals; and the kitchen island, made of butcher block, marble or Corian, and usually surrounded by stools. Each of these dining areas had, in its turn, created entire industries. There were magazines dedicated to describing and picturing "eat-in" kitchens. Volumes had been written on breakfast rooms. We had one, although no one could ever convince Justin that it was worth our while to spend two years building a room where he could eat Frosted Flakes.

So there we were. The modern American family, in the all-American home, poised for a Chinese takeout meal. At dinner, I learned that nothing happened at school, that all the decorators were sure Barry did it but that I would get him off, and that Maria had opened a charge account at Bloomingdale's and needed me to cosign. I knew I would never last until the evening news. That night, I went gently.

But even the deadest sleep can produce the liveliest nightmare. Soon after I closed my eyes, Barry appeared. He was in the witness box. I'd never seen him look this way. He wore a white flowing robe and sandals. He had grown a beard and there were thin branches with thorns on his head. I knew this look from somewhere. I couldn't place it, but my impression was that it was very bad karma. I wanted to yell out, "Barry! Who dressed you? What happened to charcoal gray?" But I was rooted to my chair at the defense counsel table. I sat silently as the prosecutor approached my client. The prosecutor looked familiar as well. He was dressed in a pilgrim costume. I couldn't see the judge; the bench was hidden in fog. From the fog a voice intoned, "You may begin, Mr. Mather." The name fit the face—the prosecutor was Cotton Mather, late of Salem witch trial fame.

"State your name," Mather began.

"Barry Stapleton."

"Your address."

"Thirty-two Marlboro Street, Boston."

"Did you know Bruno?"

"We were partners."

"When did he die?"

"Bruno died today. Or was it yesterday?"

I was on my feet. "Objection, Your Honor. Camusian dilemma, clearly irrelevant. Existential hearsay."

"Overruled. The prosecution will continue."

"You are an interior decorator, sir?"

"Yes." At that answer, a gasp came from the side where the jury would normally sit. I looked and saw a group of people staring at Barry with pure hatred in their eyes. The jurors were all holding items or had things on the floor next to them. The array of personal property included broken louvered blinds, streaked and misprinted wallpapers, and velvet paintings of cats with big eyes. There was a hand-painted screen with colors that didn't match. *Trompe l'oeil* that didn't fool anyone. End tables that were of different heights. One woman juror held a stack of bills which were each marked "overpriced" in red. Another juror, a fat little lady, jumped up shaking her fist. "He's a decorator! String him up!"

"Not yet, madam," intoned the faceless judge. "As I told you before: first the trial, and then we string him up. You may continue, Mr. Mather."

"As a decorator, sir, is it true that you regularly promise delivery of merchandise to your clients on a date that is often weeks or months before the goods actually arrive?"

"I object!" I was on my feet. "This is highly prejudicial. And besides, it's usually the manufacturer's fault. Or at least the trucking company's."

"Overruled. The witness will answer."

"Yes."

"And is it true that you often charge your clients double or triple what antiques actually cost you?"

"Your Honor, I object. Ladies and gentlemen of the jury," I said, turning toward them, "isn't a decorator entitled to make a living?"

The judge said, "Overruled." But what troubled me more was that several of the jurors appeared to be cleaning pistols or sharpening knives.

"The witness will answer," said the judge.

"Yes," said my client.

"I rest," said the prosecutor.

"Guilty," said the jury.

"Nail him to the cross," said the judge.

And that's what the whole group of them proceeded to do. But in my dream it was a faux cross with faux nails. So the enraged jurors kept raising him up and he kept sliding down. Over and over.

I began to toss and turn. "Stop!" I yelled. "Enough, enough, enough...." Someone was shaking me. I bolted upright and saw Ally next to me.

"Enough what?" she said.

"Ally. I've had the most incredible nightmare. It makes Nicely Nicely Johnson's look like a fun boat ride. Barry's in big trouble. I'm not sure an interior designer could ever get a fair trial in this country. Child molesters, yes," I said, sitting up, "but decorators—never."

"So, tell me," said Ally as she carelessly ran a finger across my chest. "Have you really had enough?"

It turned out that I hadn't. I'd trade erotic for neurotic most any night.

DON'T FORGET

When you have oak floors pickled, the first coat of polyurethane should be high gloss, which provides a hard surface. The next two coats can be a matte finish.

TEN

The next morning Allyn lay in bed and only Justin and I appeared in the breakfast room. I poured the cereal while he poured the juice. I sat across from him and just stared. It's a funny thing. You grow up and go to college getting ready for a career and thinking about marriage. These things can be planned and imagined. But it's really impossible to imagine what it's like to have your own child, sitting across from you, growing and changing while your own life develops. It's like a play within a play.

"So, what's happening this year?" I began. "It can't always be 'nothing.'"

"Oh Dad, you know I just say that to torture you."

"Enough torture," I said. "I've got clients for that. From you I expect better."

"Okay. How's this? I despise soccer."

"That's not a crime."

"I can't tell any of my friends. They all like it. You run around and get kicked in the shins and pushed. If you're lucky, you get to hit the ball with your head, and you know what's worse?"

"Tell me."

"The coach is a fascist."

"Mr. Altry?"

"Absolutely. All he talks about is the team. Love the team. Sacrifice for the team. What about the individual?"

"Any individual in particular?"

"Me. I hate the game."

"Should I come to the next one?"

"Sure, maybe I'll score."

"And then?"

"Then I'd love the game. But Altry would still be a fascist. How's your case?"

"I'm making progress."

"Any dictators?"

"No, just decorators. What's with the fascist fascination?"

"History."

"Aha!" I shouted. "I knew you were learning something."

"Now can I go back to saying 'nothing' when you ask me what's new?"

"One week," I offered.

"Make it three."

"I'm a lawyer, settle for two."

"It's a deal," he said as I tried to give him a hug. He gave me a look and we were off to school.

I dropped Justin off and headed for work. Ally was meeting a client for breakfast at the Four Seasons Hotel and I had told her I'd stop by and say hello. In the midst of her Show House preparations, she was contacted by the personal assistant to a Hollywood big-shot producer named Steve Ashworth. I seemed to remember his name in connection with some big-budget action flicks that obviously added more to his net worth than to the cultural evolution of the western world. The good news was that he had plunked down sixteen million for a summer cottage in Nantucket, and he was in town to sign up his new decorator. Ironically, he once worked with Megan, but as she was a bit interrupted, he had made a few calls and hired Ally.

When I heard Ally talking to him on the phone, I invited myself to their breakfast meeting. I had nothing to add to the decorating palaver, but as I understood that Ashworth had already spent time with Bruno and Barry, perhaps he had some observations about my client and his alleged victim which could be helpful. So I pulled up to the hotel, gave my car to the valet, and headed inside to the Bristol lounge to meet my beloved and her prey.

Ally was seated at a table, and I walked over and sat down next to her on the banquette.

"Not a moment too soon," she said out of the side of her mouth as I sat down. "Something L.A. this way cometh."

I looked toward the front of the room. A short, pudgy, forty-something guy was entering. He had a terrific tan, a power ponytail, and was talking on a cell phone. He looked our way and waved at Ally.

"Gee," I said, looking around at the other, more traditional Boston breakfast eaters. "He was tough to spot."

"Be nice," Ally said, as she waved him over.

Steve walked toward us, all the while talking away on his cell phone. He was obviously becoming angry during the conversation, as he kept jabbing at the air and gesticulating with his free hand. The last words I heard him say before sitting down at our table were, "I'm telling you, Schindler's pissed!" He slammed the phone closed and glared at me. To break the tension, and assuming I had heard wrong, I chimed in, "Great movie."

Ashworth continued to stare at me as if in a daze. Just as quickly, he leaned forward, looking at me. "What are you talking about?" he asked.

"*Schindler's List*," I said. "Great movie."

"What great movie?" He continued, "I'm telling you Schindler's pissed. Morty Schindler, head of the studio. He saw the budget, and I'm telling you he's pissed." Then he stared at me again. "Who the hell are you anyway?"

"Pay no attention to him, Steven," said Ally coming to my rescue. "He's my first husband." Some rescue. It was time to save myself.

"Great to meet you, Steve," I said standing up and offering my hand for an obligatory shake. I turned to my wife. "Allyn darling, perhaps I should leave you two to talk decorating. I've got a big day, so I'll pass on a long breakfast." At this point, I leaned toward her and lowered my voice, "Try not to get Steven pissed."

Ashworth, who had sunk back into his chair in some kind of a trance, bolted upright as I whispered to Ally. He looked at me nervously. "Steven's pissed?" he asked.

"You are?" I was now thoroughly confused.

"Not me," he said, as his eyes darted around the room. "You know, Steven."

I continued to look at him blankly.

He lowered his head and whispered, "Steven, you know, Spielberg."

"Why would Spielberg be pissed at you?" I asked.

Here he became apoplectic. "Shhh! Shhh! Not so loud. If people knew that Spielberg was pissed at me it would ruin my career."

"Is he?" I asked, growing increasingly befuddled by the man in front of me, who was now sweating profusely, his eyes darting around like a cornered weasel.

"Why, what have you heard?"

"Nothing," I said.

"What about you?" He looked imploringly at Ally.

"Ditto," she said in her most reassuring manner.

"Shit! This is terrible," he said, jumping up from the table. "I gotta go back to my room and call the coast. I got an agent, a manager, three lawyers, and a PR firm. And I have to hear this from you. Let me tell you, questions are going to be asked." He leaned down, kissed Ally's cheek and, uttering the perfunctory "later, babe," rushed out of the Bristol Lounge, toward the elevators and beyond.

"So, how do you like my new client?" Ally asked.

"How's his taste?"

"I think it's safe to say he personifies every cliché of an L.A. movie mogul."

"So, not too bright, typically insecure, and has *beaucoup d'argent*. Sounds like an unlimited budget."

"Which," said Ally, "we'll probably exceed."

"Hooray for Hollywood," I said leaning over to kiss her and whisper, "Later, babe." She stuck out her tongue. Very elegant. "If you do actually talk to this guy, steer the conversation to Megan. Maybe he knows something."

"I'm sure most of our time will be spent on color schemes, but I'll see what I can do." She air kissed me off, and I headed for my car and the office.

ELEVEN

Despite the comedic non-breakfast break, I was at work by eight thirty. I hadn't had a chance to draft any memos to my litigation associates so that we could begin our Sherman-like march on behalf of yesterday's damsels, I was meeting with Barry, and the partners wanted me to meet with them at nine to talk business. Truth be told, I was perfectly happy to have *someone* worried about the bottom line, as long as it wasn't me. I would have to once again escape the business meeting.

The trouble is that the law, noble profession though it may be, is one lousy business. Most of us come out of law school expecting to argue precedent-breaking cases in the Supreme Court. Instead, we end up worrying about overhead, trying to extract retainers, and attempting to bill more hours than anyone else. Our only inventory is our clients. What other business has so fickle and demanding an inventory? At least when a dentist goes out of business he has some equipment and unused gold to sell. All we have is our good names and no buyers. That's why we have to gather our rosebuds while we can, and partners' meetings are an essential part of those gleanings. As luck would have it, my cast of morning characters was assembling early, so I was spared from the agony, though not necessarily by the ecstasy.

No decent criminal defense can be mounted without solid detective work. Strange as it may seem, the police are not neutral enforcers of the law. Once they pick up the scent, their job becomes essentially about making an arrest and getting a conviction. This often leads to the surprising appearance of damaging witnesses and testimony, and the mysterious disappearance of exculpatory evidence. Criminal law operates in a simple world—the prosecutors and police try to put people in jail, my minions and I try to keep them out. The costs to society of this struggle are significant. If they win more often than I, the jails become crowded with innocent people, my practice goes to hell, and my son goes to public school. But if I win more often than they, it is the street that becomes crowded with innocent people and I get to go to Nantucket again next summer. This is how the struggle between good and evil is played out in post-Biblical times.

My favorite private eye was waiting for me in my office. Peter Stromberg had nothing in common with any TV detective. He wasn't rugged or handsome. He wasn't tough or sexy. In fact, he wasn't much of anything. He was of average height, had no distinguishing physical characteristics, and wasn't much of a conversationalist. He could spend an evening in a room full of people, and the next day none of them would remember him being there. Even worse, it was often reported that when he entered a room it seemed as though someone had just left. He probably wasn't much of a date, but he was one great detective. He had found me lost witnesses, eye-witnesses and Jehovah's witnesses. Unlike every TV stiff from Paul Drake to Spenser, he was the real thing. I told Peter everything that Barry had told me and filled him in on all the events of the previous day.

Barry Stapleton arrived at nine thirty. Dark circles were already forming under his eyes. He had obviously spent the night wide-awake and worried. He wore black pants, a black raw silk double-breasted blazer, and a black shirt. I guess he was in mourning. With a cape, he could pass for a disco Zorro. I chose to keep this observation to myself.

"Let's get started," I said. "Barry, I've made a list of the allegations and the alligators." I sometimes find it helpful to use Amos 'n Andy lines to break the tension. Nothing broke, so I continued. "We're going to go through them and see what you can tell us that helps. Then we'll review, find our leads, and work on our defense. To begin with, they say you were harassing Megan."

"Maybe I was. Bruno and I had been together for years and I thought it would last forever. To find out he was unfaithful—and with a woman! I couldn't believe it. I confronted him that night. He was furious. Screamed at me to mind my own business. Told me that if I told anyone about what I knew, someone could get seriously hurt. He said it wasn't what I thought."

"What do you think he meant by that?"

"Just stupid denial, I guess. In any event, I was miserable. I stayed home for two days, with the whole thing eating away at me. Finally I called Megan. I told her I knew she was having an affair with Bruno and I told her to leave him alone. She laughed at me."

"Did she say anything?"

"Yeah. She said they were going to be partners and that she could do more for Bruno than I could, in every way. Then she hung up. I called her over and over. Sometimes she'd laugh at me, sometimes she'd just hang up. I even wrote her stupid little notes. Things like, 'Please leave Bruno alone.' I disgusted myself."

"The prosecutor made a big deal out of a scene at a restaurant. What happened?"

"A couple of days before they were attacked, I stopped in at Excelsior for a drink at around five o'clock.

They have a few little tables in the bar area. Megan and Bruno were sitting together. I watched them. They were whispering and laughing together. I lost it. I ran over to the table. The whole thing seems a blur—I told them I couldn't stand it anymore, that they'd be sorry—something like that."

"Did you threaten to kill anyone?"

"Who knows? I certainly felt that way."

"Then what?"

"I went home and stayed there for the next two days. At some point, I realized that I was going to have to survive and work. We had some ideas about rooms at Show House, so I packed my briefcase and went over. You know, the Show House must go on."

"What happened at Show House?" I asked.

"I arrived around the same time as everyone else. We were walking around and talking. I asked someone, I don't remember who, if they'd seen Bruno. No one had any memory of seeing him, so I thought I'd go upstairs to look. After all, we were supposed to be partners working on a room together. I was walking around, thinking, not paying too much attention to anything when people started screaming. There was a confused mob scene and then I heard someone shouting that Megan had been killed. I had a terrible feeling, maybe a premonition, and I had to find Bruno. While everyone was huddled around the body, I went upstairs. It took me a while, I don't know how long, because I looked in all the rooms on the second and third floors. Finally, I came to the fourth floor. I heard water dripping from one of the rooms and went there first."

Barry began to shake, but Stromberg told him to go on.

"I walked into the bathroom and...it was the most awful thing I'd ever seen. I just stared and stared—I couldn't move. What I did next is a blur. I think I turned, walked down the stairs and went home. I'm not even sure how I got home. But I got into bed and just lay there looking at the ceiling. Then the police came."

"Barry," I asked, "did you hear or see anything on the fourth floor? Did you see anyone on the way up? Did you hear anything?"

"Nothing."

"Look," I said, "we've got to develop a direction that points away from you. Other than Bruno's relationship with Megan, was there anything else unusual about him or his activities that you noticed in the last month or so?"

"Nothing."

"'Nothing' won't work. We need something. I remember when Ally was describing the discovery of Megan to me, she mentioned a few people who were with her: Melissa, Frankie and some guy in the fine art business."

"Johnny Bishop. Bishop of Boston Fine Arts."

"Right. That's the one. Do you think there's something in that group?"

"Who knows? Melissa's some ditzy decorator's assistant. I doubt she even knew Bruno. Frankie's a crook, but I can't imagine he'd kill anyone."

"What do you mean, crook?"

"He has a drapery studio and does the finest work in the city. We used to be a big customer of his."

"Used to be? Tell me more."

"The way we work when we do window treatments is that we pick out a fabric, get the client's approval and then call in Frankie to measure, so we know how much to order. One day Bruno was having lunch in Chinatown with a client. After lunch, just for fun, they walked around the area that has discount fabric stores. They're in one store, and the client is laughing and asking Bruno why we can't get him material at these low prices. Bruno is trying to explain the difference between real silk and real schlock and demonstrating as he speaks by pulling out bolts of mediocre material. Mediocre that is, until he pulls out a roll of the identical fabric that we had used for that client's drapes at half the price we'd paid for the same thing. Bruno told me the client started fuming on the spot, and when he promised a refund the client stormed off."

"And what does this have to do with Frankie?"

"Bruno worked like a madman pulling out all the fabric in the store. It was loaded with expensive material. He confronted the owner, who was only too happy to tell him that he bought it from Frankie."

"I take it Frankie was over-measuring and selling off the extra."

"Exactly. And, when you think about it, that could be a lot of extra. He had a national business."

"What did you do about it?"

"Honestly, I don't know. The last time I asked Bruno, he told me he was negotiating with Frankie. Then he winked and said, 'Cha-ching, cha-ching.'"

"The sound of a cash register?"

"The very same. I used to leave those things to Bruno. Now I don't know what I'm going to do."

"Hopefully not end up like Bruno. Anyway, Frankie's on my list. What about Johnny?"

"In my opinion, a vile creature."

"Vile," I said. "Now you're talking. Vile could be good."

"Believe me, there was nothing good about him, except for his art. He was a great source for old masters, Hudson River School, Impressionist—that sort of thing. Many of our clients look at great art as part of a decorating scheme. If the room is blue, they want Matisse. We once had an order for a green Van Gogh. You can't imagine the philistines we have to put up with to make a living."

Somehow I could, but I let the irony lie where it lay.

"But let me tell you," Barry continued, "every time there's an article in the paper about stolen art, forgeries, or even the Gardener Museum heist, I expect to see his name.

"Only last week I had picked up a Renoir on approval for a very good client. Johnny told us he bought it from a Swiss dealer, whose father bought it from its original owner. He claimed that it had been out of public view for over a hundred years. Well, it seems that the client hung the painting at his home over a weekend when his wife was hosting a dinner party for the French Library. One of the guests was a museum curator from Paris, and he swore that the painting was on a list of art looted by the Nazis. The painting's title that was on the frame was unfamiliar to him, but he swore this painting fit a description he knew, and that someone had changed the name. As I understand it, the client was mortified. He canceled all of our remaining work. Bruno said he was going to ruin Bishop."

Saying that, Barry opened his mouth in amazement and stared at me. "Do you think it's possible?"

"I'm hoping for probable," I responded.

"You're forgetting Megan," said Stromberg, who was sitting quietly as Barry and I talked. "Bishop was the one who gave her mouth-to-mouth and may have saved her life."

"Listen," I said "One victim at a time. At least we've got something to look at. I still want to look at the business angle first. We'll get to Frankie and Bishop in due course. Take Stromberg with you to your office and apartment. I want him to go through all of Bruno's things. Where are the books and records of the decorating business?"

"Bruno was in charge of all that. He kept the books at our place."

"Stromberg, go through the records. Money's supposed to be the root of all evil. So go find some evil. Call me at the end of the day with good news."

They left, my faithful gumshoe leading a forlorn soul dressed in black. I put my feet up on the desk and looked out over the harbor. I needed inspiration. I called Allyn. She wasn't home, so I called her cell phone.

"Hello, sweets. Do you miss me in the worst way?" I asked when she picked up the phone.

"I don't know. What's the best way?"

I was stumped. "No time for Zen conundrums, kiddo. I need help. I've got to find an angle on the Stapleton case. Bruno and Megan were up to something. Who knows everything about everything in the decorating business? I need a major league gossip."

"This one's so easy my only charge will be a few moments of manual labor. I'm on my way to the Show House and I'll give you my ideas while you carry a few things out of the car. See you."

Allyn's offer of help sounded good, although I knew her well enough to be worried about the few moments of labor. She would have been a great Pharaoh. I could see her telling the tribes of Israel not to worry, "It's only a small pyramid." On the other hand, she never would have made it past frogs, let alone lice and boils. I decided to save my strength and take a cab to the Promised Land.

My cab reached Louisburg Square just as Ally was pulling up in front of the Show House. My driver maneuvered in behind Ally's Rover. I got out and walked around to the driver's side as Ally was lowering the tailgate. Two very large granite dogs stared out at me.

"I can't lift those!" I yelled to Ally as she was walking into the house. She waved and entered.

I turned back to the driver, who was waiting patiently. "How'd you like to make an extra twenty by carrying those little dogs inside?"

"I am cab driver, not carrier," he responded quickly in a deep Russian accent. "In Odessa, I was metallurgist. My wife was computer software engineer. Now in this land of opportunity my son has full scholarship to Cornell, my wife works in bagel bakery and I drive taxi."

"Okay, forty," I responded.

"Make it fifty, and I only help."

"Deal," I said quickly.

"I love America," my proud metallurgist stated as he got out of the cab and took my fifty dollars.

Together, with a great deal of huffing and puffing, we managed to haul the two mastiffs into the living room. My nouveau capitalist assistant, now somewhat stooped, left in a blaze of more "oys" and "gevalts" than had ever been uttered in all of fair Louisburg Square, let alone this living room. I took off my jacket and flopped on the window seat.

Ally, looking fresh and well tailored, stood by the fireplace, a dog on each side. "Don't you think they look good here, darling?"

"Even better if they'd trotted in by themselves." I caught my breath and surveyed the room—it was beginning to look like Allyn was having her way with it.

"Very nice," I said. "What's it going to be?"

"Taupe and beige, soft blues. Silk and taffeta curtains. A lot of hand painting, Aubusson rug, drop-dead artwork."

"How's the rest of the place look?"

"It's getting there. Go take a look around. Introduce yourself. Make friends. Maybe you'll find a lead. I have to wait for some workmen."

I accepted the invitation for a stroll and walked out of Ally's living room into the great front hall. The last time I'd been in this room it had been crowded with police, distraught Leaguers, and mauled decorators. Today, there were serious men and women with clipboards. Carpenters and wallpaper hangers were passing by, coming and going from rooms. I saw two familiar middle-aged women in jeans and sweatshirts walk by me. I would have said hello, but they were too engrossed in conversation to notice me.

"I'm not happy with the dust ruffle, Anne. I'm not happy."

"Listen, Judy, I'm not too thrilled with the sconces."

Not exactly food for my table. I turned my attention

to a woman sitting at a card table who was waving me over. She gave off the aura of one who is definitely in charge. Full-figured, as we say in these politically correct times, and frowning, she tapped a pen on the clipboard that was on the table in front of her. Obviously she was the Show House mother.

"All workmen must sign in. You should know the rules," she intoned with the haughty diction of one who usually has others speak to workmen for her. I thought I'd warm up to her by showing our social bond.

"I'm not really a workman. I'm just a man who for the moment appears to be working. It happens in the best of families."

Although she was sitting below me, and I was standing above, I still got the feeling that she was looking down her nose at me. She stared. I signed.

I wandered the house, looking in rooms to see painters painting, plumbers plumbing and carpenters... carpenting. My early life had not prepared me to be of any assistance to or have any appreciation for this type of activity. I remember being on the junior prom decorating committee, and making hundreds of tin foil stars to hang up in the gym in order to transform the place from sweat box to "Some Enchanted Evening." When we were through, I'm sure the place looked exactly like a gymnasium covered in tinfoil.

The Show House was going through a more dramatic transformation, made all the more so by the fact that a couple of dozen prima donnas were working under the same roof in competition to produce the "best" room. Over the years, I had devised a prima donna rating system. The tens were easy. Usually the doors to their rooms were kept closed so that their schemes would remain secret, as if they were the Russians working on Sputnik while hiding from U2 spy planes. At the other end of the spectrum, I am proud to proclaim, was my spouse. She was friendly, courteous, kind, and obeyed the law of the pack—a regular Boy Scout of designers. If only she carried her own dogs.

I was clearly out of place as I wandered the halls. Everyone seemed to be doing something. Complaining was very popular. Someone named Carl had tracked his mess through Julia's room. Julia was no good because she wouldn't tell Noreen the name of her painter. And Noreen's electrician had blown the fuses in Bruce's bathroom. I checked out the aforesaid *salle de bain*, which was decorated with horses and hunt scenes. What did these people think went on in bathrooms? Maybe Beacon Hill was like TV in the fifties, when you couldn't say the word toilet. "Where are you going, dear?" "To the hunt, mater."

I'd had enough. No sense ruining the surprises of opening night. I walked back to Ally's room. She was supervising curtain installers, and I saw that if I moved fast I could get out before she found something for me to do.

"Okay, kid, I carried the dogs. Pay-off time."

"You work cheap, Buzz. I hope you do better with your clients. Just walk down the street to Farcus and Company. Beth Farcus is expecting you." Then she turned back to the work at hand. "Maria, that pole is much too low."

Making sure to sign out, I was on my way to find Farcus.

TWELVE

Charles Street, as yuppified as any street in America, was at the foot of Beacon Hill, dividing the Hill from the Back Bay. There were several greengrocers and wine stores, each specializing in what's new, chic, and in. Its quaint bistros and trendy restaurants all featured nouvelle pizzas, which were usually inedible. Whoever discovered goat cheese should be exiled, especially if it was the same guy who decided to put it on pizzas in the spot where pepperoni was supposed to be. For my money, let goat cheese melt in Wolfgang Puck's mouth, where it belongs. It doesn't travel well.

Charles Street is also home to a bevy of antiquaries, all top-drawer and all top-dollar. Farcus and Company was one of those. I pushed the doorbell, tried to look like a buyer and not a mugger, and was buzzed entrance.

Whenever I enter a very classy English antique store, which this obviously was, I am struck by the same thought. In the first half of the eighteenth century, there were only thirty-five thousand upper-class homes in England. Assume, for the sake of my problem, that each one of them had only one dining room. This would account for one dining room table and one sideboard per home. Assuming reasonable wear and tear over the last two hundred years, the majority of these pieces had to have fallen apart by now. And yet, as I've traveled the highways of New England, and have been dragged into every driveway, garage, or grass path that had an antique sign hanging over it, I believe I have seen enough authentic antique dining room tables and sideboards to allow for one per person in eighteenth century England, with plenty left over for the colonies. That's a real mystery. Farcus and Company had its share, though, and the furniture pieces were rather nice.

The woman coming toward me must have been the owner because not too many of the hired help wear Chanel to work these days. Does it tell you something about my home life that I can identify designer clothes? With a reputation as "The Source," I expected Ms. Farcus to be something on the order of Yenta the Matchmaker. What I got instead was slinky elegance far more à la mode New York than Beacon Hill. She had jet black hair that hung loose to her shoulders, the topper to an athletic body. She was my age, but with a fresh tight face that was as much a tribute to her plastic surgeon as to her own good health regimen. I could see why people would open up to her, but I was sure the opening of their souls was just a prelude to the opening of their wallets.

"I'm Beth Farcus," she breathed, "and I bet you're Buzz Levin."

"I'd like to think that my stellar reputation precedes me, but my guess is my wife called."

"And she told me that you were such a dear man that I was to give you all the help I could. Barry is a good friend and a great customer. Guilty or innocent, I want that man on the street, especially Charles Street. I'll help any way I can."

"I'm sure you know all about the fights between Barry and Bruno, Barry's jealousy, Bruno's involvement with Megan. I just don't believe that after years of living gaily ever after, Bruno decided to give the girls a chance. And of all girls, Megan."

"Why, you really are an old-fashioned boy, aren't you? But you may be right. Megan was a user of the highest order. She could close her eyes, see dollar signs and screw anyone—even Bruno. What he'd want with her is more difficult to figure out. Maybe he just wanted to see what it was like to make love while looking into someone's eyes for a change." She winked at me, as if to see if I caught her ever-so-risqué drift. I winked back. It was either that, or tell her what a jerk she was, which would probably end her usefulness as an informational font.

"Here's an odd tidbit, though," she went on. "Three months ago, I sold Bruno an armoire for a client of his. He paid me with a twenty-thousand-dollar check, and three days later, my own dear little personal banker called to tell me that the check had bounced. Well, I've done business with Barry and Bruno for years so I assumed it was some kind of mix up. I asked my man to put it through again. Three days later, déjà bounce. I called Bruno, who was very apologetic, said there had been computer problems and that he would take care of it right away. That afternoon Megan comes in, reaches into a lovely skin purse, hands me four packs of hundred-dollar bills, five thousand dollars to a pack, tells me it's from Bruno, cheerio, can't stop to talk, and she's out the door."

"Did you ever ask Bruno about it?"

"Never had a chance. Never saw him again. Later, the gossip started about some link between Bruno and Megan. They were seen at dinner. Someone saw them in New York. A sighting in Palm Beach. Well, I thought, there's certainly more in heaven and earth than my science ever dreamt of, and the next thing you know, one's dead and the other's comatose. Listen, I hope Barry gets off, but if you ask me, he did it. Hell hath no fury like a woman scorned, or whatever."

"Do me a favor," I said. "Don't volunteer for the jury. One last thing: Those bounced checks make me wonder—how was Bruno and Barry's business?"

"I always thought they were top of the heap. Barry had great taste and Bruno kept signing up clients. Take that armoire they bought for twenty thousand dollars. They'd probably spend a couple of thousand dollars cleaning it up and then resell it somewhere else for fifty thousand. Those boys were rich, believe me."

"One more 'last' question. What can you tell me about Johnny Bishop?"

"Johnny? I think the world of him. What does he have to do with all this?"

"Maybe nothing. He was at the Show House when Megan and Bruno were found."

"That's odd."

"What is?"

"That he was at the Show House. He sells to decorators, he wouldn't be trying to do a room himself. I guess," she said, pushing back the hair that had fallen in front of her eyes, "that he was looking for business. But it still seems odd."

Odd was not as good as vile. But together they presented possibilities. I continued, "What do you know about his business reputation?"

"When it comes to fine art, he is simply the best. He must have incredible sources."

"If he were accused of selling stolen art, how would it affect him?"

"First of all, I wouldn't believe it of him. But, and I say this hypothetically, if he were, he'd be in a real bind. Years ago, it didn't really matter where art came from. Some of the greatest pieces in the world were stolen. You can start with the Elgin Marbles and count forward. But those days are over, especially in fine art. Now if a painting's provenance is not impeccable, it won't be touched."

"And," I asked, "if it got out that he was peddling a Renoir that may once have been acquired by the Third Reich for less than fair market value?"

"If he were accused and it were true, his next art sale would be of a big-eyed cat on velvet at Kmart."

She obviously saw the satisfied look on my face, so she added, "But believe me, it couldn't be true."

"I do believe you. And thanks for all the information. Getting back to Megan and Bruno, you've added the factor of a bag of cash to a scenario that previously only had sex and jealousy. Sex, plus cash, plus jealousy: Now we've got everything." I shook her hand and turned to leave. An older man with a much younger woman was entering the store. She was exuding excitement as she looked around; he appeared to be resigned to his fate. I recognized him as the recently divorced vice president of a State Street venture capital firm. This, too, was sex plus cash, but today this deadly combination appeared destined for antiques, not homicide. As I walked out to the street, I knew that Farcus and Company was about to have a better day than I was having.

I felt a tingling in my chest. It was either my heart going into spasm from the day's chores, or my cell phone, carried in the breast pocket of my jacket, was vibrating. I reached for the phone. My dislike for cell phones is well known. When they began appearing in pockets, that dislike turned to hatred. There is no mystery and little romance in a world where everyone is just a push button away. Would it have been a better world if Mrs. Livingston had kept calling Stanley to ask if he had found her husband yet? Or if Edmund Hillary's mother called him every morning to remind him to button his coat because it got cold on top of Mount Everest? No matter what he was doing, he would have had to answer. And so did I.

The news wasn't good and I turned back up Beacon Hill, this time at a gallop. When I reached the Show House there were several people milling about on the front steps where Ally was sitting, bricks and hunks of cement strewn around her.

"Allyn," I panted. "What happened? Are you okay?"

"Shaken, but nothing broken. I came out to get some fresh air. I was standing on the steps looking at a couple of fabric swatches. I still wasn't quite sure about that green. The beige in the rug looked different in artificial light."

"Allyn, the accident."

"Right. I was holding up pieces of fabric in the sunlight when one fell out of my hands and started blowing away. I took a couple of steps to reach it when, kaboom."

"Kaboom?"

"Just like in the cartoons," she said, pointing out the fallen debris. "No sooner had I moved when all this stuff came rolling off the roof and landed where I had just been standing."

She was giving bravery her best shot. But I walked over and hugged her as tears rolled down her cheeks. I kissed her tears and held her. One of the workmen came out of the house.

"I went up on the roof," he said. "Looks like the wind knocked off the top of the chimney."

I picked up one of Ally's fabrics and held it out. There was a soft rustle of cloth from the gentle breeze. "Wind, my ass. Stay out here while I check something inside," I said, unwrapping my arms and walking in the front door. I went over to the table where I had previously signed in. The matron at arms was absent and I grabbed the clipboard, scanning it for familiar names.

Suspects came falling off the page. There was a sign-in for Mr. Ashworth and friend as well as Frankie and Johnny. I suppose they could all explain their presence. It was finding Barry's name on the list that was somewhat disconcerting. He was supposed to be helping Stromberg. Had I misjudged him? Was he crazy enough to be out attacking decorators and was I crazy to be representing him? *Both important questions*, I thought, as I walked outside.

"Ally, come with me, I'm taking you home."

"Don't be ridiculous," she said, standing up and walking to the door. "I'm okay. Accidents happen. All's well that ends well. Yadda, yadda, yadda."

"'Yadda' my ass. People are in danger at this house and I'm not leaving you here."

"I know you're worried. Believe me, *I'm* worried. But I'll go inside where there are plenty of people. I won't be alone. If I go home and just sit, well, then I guarantee you I'll go to pieces." She kissed me on both cheeks, appearing brave, but then pulling me close and holding me tightly to her. Now my heart wasn't the only part of me that was palpitating. Ally held me closer, and whispered in my ear, "This is either going to be one very kinky and public scene, or perhaps your phone is ringing." She stepped back, waved, and walked through the door.

I was befuddled, then bemused when I discovered that my phone, which I had replaced in my pants' left front pocket was humming away. I pulled it out and answered. It was Stromberg. He informed me that if I met him at Grille 23 and bought him a steak for lunch, he would enlighten me.

I told him I would and that I had a few tidbits for him as well. The day was still nice and I seized this new opportunity to walk off recent distress. The longer this case went, the more likely it was that I could get in shape. I headed away from the Hill, back down to Charles Street and out across Beacon Street. Although not exactly Hollywood and Vine, this corner is well known to viewers of *Cheers*. I cut between the Public Gardens and The Commons, turned a couple of corners and arrived at Grille 23 just as Stromberg was entering.

We sat and ordered. Peter, obviously unimpressed with the current movement away from cholesterol and red meat, ordered a large steak, well done, with mashed potatoes. I settled for grilled chicken. The waiter had neither told us his name nor announced any specials. I had high hopes for the rest of the meal.

"It'll be a while until they burn your steak to perfection, Peter, so give me a summary of your investigating."

"As instructed, I went to the apartment. Bruno kept his office there. It doesn't look like he was much of a bookkeeper. Bank statements were unopened, there was no general ledger, and paid bills and receipts were nonexistent. I made myself comfortable and opened all of his mail and bank statements. In the last six months, about eleven million dollars had moved in and out of the account. There were no deposit slips or records of the receipt of money. Strangely enough, each month the account was drawn down to zero. A number of checks showed up as written to various wholesale suppliers, and checks were written to Barry and Bruno. It appeared that of the eleven million, however, Bruno and Barry had drawn about two hundred thousand dollars, and all the rest was paid to suppliers. One supplier that kept appearing was Claridge and Sons. They're factory reps for rugs, furniture, fabric, and wall coverings. Of the eleven million dollars received, Claridge had been paid nine and a half million bucks."

"Not a bad beginning," I said.

"Well," Stromberg added, "I've still got some work to do on the files. There were lots of checks without any entries, so I'll spend some time going over them to see if anything interesting pops up."

I knew that decorators like Bruno and Barry marked up products by at least one hundred percent. All the wholesalers marked their products with a code, usually the 7-11 system. It was easy. If Bruno had a client who was looking for a sofa, he could bring her to Claridge to look and shop. The sofa the client might see and like would be marked 57-22. Subtract 7 from the 57 and 11 from 22 and Bruno's cost would be $5,011. He would then quote the client at least $10,022 before moving on to find fabric, similarly marked, to cover the couch. With this markup, whatever amount Bruno paid the wholesaler, he paid himself and Barry the same. Therefore, if Bruno had paid Claridge over nine million dollars, then he and Barry should have taken in about nine million for themselves. Peter had asked Barry about the accounts and payments and Barry was baffled. He said that during the last few months, he had been too preoccupied with Bruno to pay attention to business, and he thought the cash flow was pretty meager. He had no explanation for the millions.

"Speaking of Barry," I said. "Where is he?"

"I don't know," Peter responded. "He went over to the apartment with me, then said he had to run an errand. Why?"

I ran through the day's events. "You know Peter, there's a lot of circumstantial evidence pointing to our client. He said he didn't do it, but he's sans alibi or explanation, and we don't have any other great suspects. I'll give the guy my best shot, but not if my wife is on his decorator hit list. Do me a favor, whenever you have the chance, keep an eye on our client. I'll watch my wife."

"You got it."

As Stromberg had his coffee and I paid the check, I remembered the old line from a Mouseketeer song, "Today is a day that is filled with surprises." We were actually coming up with some clues, although who knew where some of them pointed. I'd hate to find out my own client was guilty, unless it meant saving Ally. I urged Stromberg to keep on the job, maybe nose around Claridge a little. As for me, I decided to go over to the hospital and check out Megan. She may have mumbled something to a nurse. At the very least, there could be an open box of Godiva chocolates on her night table.

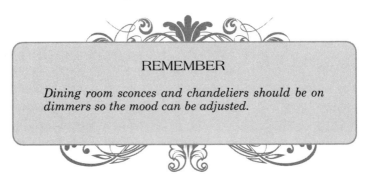

REMEMBER

Dining room sconces and chandeliers should be on dimmers so the mood can be adjusted.

THIRTEEN

There was a cabstand next to the Grille's side door, and I was able to whisk myself away to Massachusetts General Hospital, or MGH to us locals.

I suppose the walk would have done me good, but in my present state I would probably arrive at the hospital as a patient if I tried hoofing it; thus, I sought out horsepower other than my own.

I arrived at the hospital and was told that Megan was ensconced in the tenth floor of the new tower. Had Megan been conscious, I am sure she would have been proud of her accommodations. The new tower rose above what was once the Phillips House. Back in the glorious days before managed care and HMOs, the Phillips House accommodated only the finest substance abusers, malingerers and hypochondriacs of Boston society. Many of the rooms had fireplaces, and family servants were on hand to assist the nurses in doling out placebos. Truly, *la* phlegm *de la crème*.

Those days are for the most part long gone, a modern medical building now looming above the old foundation. However, glass and steel does not a true democracy make. Special patients, meaning those who can pay extra, and for more than just a remote controlled TV, are in the private rooms on the top two floors. Megan's room was on the top floor.

I took the elevator, exited by the nurses' station and walked down to Megan's room. The door was open and I peered in. She certainly appeared, as they say, to be resting comfortably. Were it not for the wires, intravenous drips, and some bells and whistles, Megan might be mistaken for a woman sound asleep with a large turban around her head. Of course, the aforementioned headgear was bandages and the sleep was a deep coma. Based on the digital readout and rising and falling line on one of the machines next to her, either her heart was working or it was a turbulent day on Wall Street.

There was a woman sitting next to her and a man sitting at the foot of the bed. The man was a bit of a surprise. I entered the room.

"Mr. Ashworth," I said. "Twice in one day. We met at the Four Seasons? Buzz Levin, Allyn's husband?"

Ashworth looked as surprised as I, and certainly less comfortable than the lifeless limbs that lay abed between us.

"Levin," he said, rising from his chair and walking away toward the window. "Small world, eh? I've known Megan for years. She decorated my place in Brentwood. Great style. But she was an impossible woman to work with, although I almost hired her again. When I bought the Nantucket place I thought of Megan, but I switched to your wife. Terrible about poor Megan, eh?"

"Let's hope for the best," I responded as I turned to the seated woman. "Hello," I said.

Ashworth jumped in. "Bunny, say hello to Buzz Levin, my decorator's husband. Bunny's an old friend from Los Angeles."

She may have been a friend, but old was not the adjective I would have chosen. She was probably in her mid-twenties. If I tell you she was gorgeous, will you think me superficial? Now Ashworth, he could afford to be superficial—he was supposed to be superficial: a short, middle-aged movie producer with a ponytail. Why was I not nonplussed to see him with a living, though fully clothed, centerfold? A particularly non-PC term, "arm candy," came to mind. Ah, the rigors of the movie business.

She rose to shake my hand. She was taller than I, with incredibly blond hair, ridiculously blue eyes, and stupendously tight clothes, which left not a lot to the imagination. "I've heard so much about your wife," she said. "We even went to the Show House to look for her today. She must have been busy because Steve couldn't find her anywhere. I hear she's wonderful."

Why do all the beautiful women I meet use the same opening line? It's less painful than ice water, but it does the trick. As for her remarks, that explains "Ashworth and friend" at the sign-in desk. Some friend.

"How old a friend are you?" I asked.

"Oh, like, not really old like old," she said, leading me to believe that I was going to have to break a valley girl code if the conversation was to continue. "Stevie was a friend of my late dad, and we, like, connected at the funeral. He's been totally wonderful to me." She looked at Ashworth, smiled and gave a slight pinky wave.

Ashworth waved his pinky back. Of course, his had a ring on it. "You may have known Bunny's father," he said, walking back to his seat. "Paul Rabitzky, he invested in a lot of my movies. His death was a terrible loss."

"Sure," I said. "He was a wonderful guy. I'm sorry." I didn't actually know Rabitzky, only of him. He was a super rich investment banker who committed suicide a couple of months ago for no apparent reason. I remembered the obituary. He left a daughter and a wife. Only a knockout like this daughter could have survived with a name like Bunny Rabitzky. Ally had told me that the wife suffered a nervous breakdown. This was a grimmer scene than I'd imagined. I decided to change the topic from the dead to the near living.

"Any change in Megan's condition?" I asked.

Bunny brightened. "Not really. But I've been totally following the doctor's orders." She smiled and held up a book.

"Visitors are supposed to read to her. It helps people in comas," Ashworth shrugged.

I looked at the book and saw that Bunny had been reading *The Celestine Prophecy* to Megan. This seemed more likely to extend a coma than complete silence would, but I didn't want to interfere with Bunny's therapy. Anyone with a name like a Russian cartoon character must know what she's doing.

"So I guess she hasn't regained consciousness or said anything," I inquired.

"Nope," said Ashworth. "She's out like a lox."

I assumed he meant "lux," the Latin word for "light" which would have been the correct end to the simile. On the other hand, she *was* just lying there.

"Too bad," I said. "You know, I'm representing the guy who's accused of all this. I had this unrealistic vision that she'd wake up, name the mugger, and my guy would go free. But I guess that only happens in movies."

"Not the good ones," said Ashworth. "In those, the criminal comes back to the hospital and finishes off the victim. Then it's a perfect crime and your guy loses."

Bunny looked at him and smiled. "Maybe we should go, Steve. I totally do not want to miss the plane." She saw my questioning look, although I doubt that's how she would have identified it. "We're going to fly over to Nantucket to see how the house is coming along."

"Sure, babe," he said. "I think this reading is a waste of time."

As if on cue, the three of us walked out of the room. A silent elevator ride lead to the front door. It was no surprise that a limo was waiting at the curb. We said brief goodbyes as I walked around the corner to find a cab. I waited a couple of minutes with no luck and, rather than waste the rest of the afternoon, decided a brisk walk was the only alternative. So I turned back around the corner, past the front door, and back up Cambridge Street toward my office. At the time, it struck me as odd that the limo was still right where I had left it a few minutes earlier and no one's head popped out of a blackened window to offer me a ride. Maybe they were too busy rereading *The Celestine Prophecy*.

FOURTEEN

You'll be happy to know, I made it back to the office, although since this whole murder/head-bashing thing, I'd walked more than in all of the last five years combined. I waved to Lisa and a few of the lawyers and walked back to my office, closed the door and curled up on the couch Allyn had been wise enough to include in my office decorations. The couch which, of course, she claims is a sofa. I remember closing my eyes.

And then I opened them. Was it the dream again? I was in my scull, but I had finally reached a dock. It was on the Charles River and led to one of the boat clubs that lined the banks. I got out and proceeded up the walkway to the back door. I tried to enter but the door was locked. I knocked and a peephole opened directly across from me. I could sense that someone was looking me over, and then the door opened and I entered.

It was unlike any boathouse I had ever seen before. The walls were red. There was a red rug on the floor, with the only furniture being large couches fit for a sultan. There were other people in the room, but they were all women, and not just any women. They were the entire female cast of a *Baywatch* repeat, attired in peignoirs, teddies, and other raiment that are the stuff of adolescent boys' and middle-aged lawyers' fantasies. I stood in the middle of the room while the women took turns winking at me, licking their lips, and generally performing suggestive hand and body signals that would have gotten Marcel Marceau an X-rating. There could be no doubt: I had wandered into my dream bordello. Either that or I had died in my sleep and was in Frederick's of Heaven.

Suddenly there were sirens, pounding at the door, and a brigade of police ran into the room. It was my old friend Lt. Daley at the head of the pack. "We've had it with prostitutes," he announced. And then, pointing at me, he yelled to his troops, "Arrest that man!"

Suddenly I was sitting alone in the back of a paddy wagon. Handcuffed and in leg irons. Visions of Jean Valjean and *The Count of Monte Cristo* flashed through my mind. A panel separating the driver from the back of the wagon slid open. I heard a familiar voice.

"Well, Levin, you've really hit bottom now. You're becoming a living lawyer joke." It was Clarence Darrow.

"Is this a dream?" I asked.

"Of course it's a dream, you schmuck. That's the problem. You're still an idealist. You still think justice will triumph. Bullshit. Remember the three Cs—cross-examination, confusion and cash. Use the first two and get the third. Now wake up. We've got a lot to do. And Levin—"

"Yes sir."

"You really should wake up. Can you imagine an actual *Baywatch* babe winking at you? Do some sit-ups. I'm in better shape than you, and I've been dead fifty years."

FIFTEEN

I woke up late in the day. Unlike one of Nero Wolf's famous dozes, my sleep had failed to produce a vision that would solve the mystery. However, my somnambulistic meandering and Clarence Darrow's kibitzing had recharged my batteries. Maybe if I could win the damn case I could dream sans Darrow. Maybe I could get back to that boathouse. Maybe barristers could fly.

Lisa gave me a note that Ally had called to invite me to the Show House after work. The League had decided that the Show House must go on, and they were holding a cocktail party to recapture some of the spirit that was understandably dampened by the crimes. I spent the rest of the afternoon paying bills and answering letters. Both acts being obligatory, I preferred to leave them for as late in the day as possible.

At seven o'clock, I presented myself at Louisburg Square, returning to the scene of the crime. Historically, these were events of incredible boredom, but the chance to mingle with potential suspects and maybe the villain him- or herself got my jurist juices flowing. Entering the living room and surveying the crowd, I decided to rule out all the members of the Women's League as suspects. They were huddled together, chatting through immovable jaws, with their husbands in attendance, drinks in hand, nodding knowledgeably. How they could talk without opening their mouths was, to me, a question of great fascination. Because this trait was found only in certain WASPish upper classes, evolutionary randomness was no explanation. It had to be an acquired characteristic. I was sure it was part of the course of instruction at Miss Porter's and other purveyors of education to the ruling class.

It was impossible to conceive of this group committing a crime of passion. Maybe a well-thought-out act of passion, but nothing criminal. *In Blue Blood* just didn't go with *In Cold Blood*. As to a premeditated sin, an aspect of this group's greatest deviance must have been the invasion of principal.

Nope. The villain was certainly a member of the decorating profession. They were temperamental, used rage as a tool of the trade, and were driven to frenzy by slightly mismatched dye-lots.

The design people milled about in their own groups in obvious contrast to the Leaguers. They were louder, the men had pant legs that actually reached their shoes, and many were eating, not just drinking. A diabolical lot. This was a much more fun crowd. But one of these merry pranksters had committed the crimes for which my client was accused, and it would help if I could figure out whom. I got a drink and waded in.

Ally saw me and waved me over. She was talking to a fellow who was dressed casually in blue velvet pants and a puffy white shirt.

"Hi, Buzz. Say hello to Lucas."

I did.

"Guess what?" Ally asked.

I couldn't. I also couldn't believe this conversational drivel, but I played along. Maybe someone would confess if I appeared friendly.

"Lucas is decorating the conservatory. He has to get through my room to get to his and we've been discussing the logistics of working together. As you know, I'm going to be doing English country and Lucas has been giving me his thoughts on a Spanish conservatory." She said this with the look in her eye that was pure ick.

"Yes," said Lucas, "I am drawn to the Spanish motif. But not some tacky Mediterranean settee. True Spanish. For me, Mr. Levin," he added, extending his arms and billowing his sleeves, "my world is that of Goya."

"You mean like white bread and trailer parks," I ventured, stealing a line from Lenny Bruce, and adding a slight "ow" as I felt Ally kick the side of my leg, while Lucas looked thoroughly confused.

"I don't follow you," Lucas said, which was okay with me. Ally was glowering in my direction, so I decided to shift out of my Leo Rosten mode. The joys of Yiddish were often wasted on the Goya.

"My mistake, old boy. How silly of me. So tell me, Lucas, who killed Bruno and almost killed Megan?"

At this conversational twist, Lucas turned a nice shade of ashen, mumbled that he had to speak to his curtain installer and hurried off.

"Brilliant work, Sherlock. I especially liked your subtle investigative technique," Ally said with a derisive twinkle in her eyes.

"Forget Lucas. His type doesn't bludgeon people to death. He bores them. Tell me, what's the gossip about the murder? Anyone got any theories?"

"The place is strangely quiet on that subject. I think everyone is trying to pretend nothing happened so that nothing else will interfere with Show House."

"Well, I'd like to meet some people and ask some questions. Who got the bathroom where Bruno was killed?"

"Wendy Winterfeld. She's the skinny one over there with the curly hair and the cheap party dress. Talking to her is no thrill, but let's give it a shot."

We ambled off in the direction of Ms. Winterfeld. She was talking to several people, all of whom seemed to be trying to move away from her. As she spoke in a high-pitched Australian whine, her audience was eyeing a table of punch and cheese puffs like convicts looking at an unguarded hole in the wall. Any second they could make their break for freedom.

"Oh hello, Ally," she waved as we got closer. Her accent was difficult to describe. She was obviously nervous in the presence of more accomplished competitors and as a result spoke a bit too fast and too high. Imagine Margaret Thatcher sucking in the gas from a helium balloon, taking speed and then speaking.

"Who's in the group with her?" I whispered.

There were two men incarcerated by Wendy's speech. One was dressed conservatively in a charcoal gray suit. He could have been a regular New England banker had he not been wearing brown suede loafers without socks. The other was in jeans and a sweater and would have passed as an average blue-collar type except for the three diamond studs in each ear. I love this crowd.

"The guy in jeans is named Gino. He owns a workroom and does window treatments. Very good. Very expensive. The man in the suit is Billy Bristol. He's the manager of Claridge and Sons. Claridge has the best wallpaper and fabrics in the Design Building and probably the best business. He's an important person to know."

Remembering Stromberg's report, I agreed that the Claridge manager was important. At that point we reached the group.

"Wendy, darling," said Ally. "Say hello to my husband, Buzz. And Buzz, say hello to Wendy, Gino and Billy." We all shook hands. Wendy looked at me as new fuel for her conversational fire.

"Oh, Buzz. I've heard all about you. You're representing Barry. Are you going to be able to get him off?"

"That depends to a large degree on whether or not he's guilty," I answered. "Any theories in this group?"

Billy answered first. "Look no further than a jealous lover. A classic triangle, Mr. Levin. I'm afraid you have a loser on your hands."

"I refuse to believe it," said Wendy. "Barry is just the nicest. I can't think of him killing anybody. I've never even seen him mad at anybody. Gino, you heard about how Paul botched an entire swag and jabot. Was Barry mad? No. I would have killed Paul. Do that to me, Gino, and you're a dead man."

This last line was more pointed than joking, and we all stared at Wendy.

"Oh, I see. Yes, of course, real murder and all. Well I'm only joking, but Barry is no killer."

I had no idea what a swag or a jabot were. Gino was giggling nervously so I assumed they were body parts.

"Don't worry love," said Gino. "Paul's a brute with shears. He couldn't get a job in home decorating at J.C. Penney."

This set off rounds of laughter. Through it all I'd done my best to direct a series of furtive glances at Billy. He was looking around the room, giving me the impression that he was hunting for an excuse to leave our little group. He found it.

"There's Bruce," he said, waving to someone across the room. "I've got to talk to him. Nice meeting you, Buzz."

"Oh, Billy," said Wendy. "A bunch of us are going over to the Ritz for a nightcap. Care to join us?"

"Sorry dear, I'd love to. Haven't been to the Ritz in years. But I'm booked for the night. Ta, all." The last was uttered with a delicate wave to the group.

"We'll talk again," I said and looked straight at Billy with my most meaningful glance. "Won't we?"

As Billy turned and left I thought I heard him mumble, "Not bloody likely." *Now, why would he say that?* I wondered.

Ally and I made some more small talk. Wendy wore us down and we, too, made a break for the cheese puffs.

"Give me a quick summary of Billy Bristol," I asked.

"Well, he lives with Bruce. But he's been rumored to be having an affair with Gino. That's his public life. In private he's *trés* bisexual. See Abigail over there? I heard that last year one of the Claridge clerks returned to the office late at night and caught a glimpse of Billy and Abigail. He was wrapped in chintz and she was *sans tout*, except, of course, her pearls and espadrilles."

"Did he have any relationship with Bruno?"

"None that I know."

"How about Megan?"

"Ditto. Why all the interest in Billy?"

"There are some Claridge facts that need explaining."

"Are you thoroughly bored yet?" asked Ally.

I was impressed by such unaccustomed concern at a decorating event. Perhaps she'd had enough of interior events and was now harboring an ulterior motive.

"Why?" I asked. "Is there any part of me that you'd like to take home, jump on and suck dry?"

She winked and held me close. "Only your wallet, big boy."

I was saved from the obligatory *ad hominem* comeback line by the booming of a loud voice behind us. "Ally, darling, you look ravishing." We both turned and I recognized Gus from previous Show Houses.

"If I ever decide to go for women," Gus said to Ally, "you will be my first." He looked over at me and continued. "How a woman of your *je ne sais quoi* can remain with The Man in The Wrinkled Flannel Suit is beyond me."

"He's not so bad," said Ally, rushing to my defense. "He's just panache impaired." Some rush.

Gus, on the other hand, was pure patina enhanced. He was tall and elegant. Six-two-ish with salt and pepper

hair, he wore handmade suits from Brioni, ties from
Charvet, and custom shirts from Turnbull. He stood with a
theatrical pose and was certainly a decorator from central
casting. Gus always carried a walking stick: tonight's had a
somewhat Greek motif. On first glance, the ivory handle
appeared to be carved with two naked boys playing
leapfrog. I passed on the second look.

"Are you doing a room this year, Gus?" I asked

"But of course, dear boy. I'm the 'Gentlemen's
Dressing Room.' A nice horsey motif. Leather, saddles,
whips. To the hunt. What a hoot. Actually, I'm expecting a
big crowd. I'm upstairs next to the bathroom *de la morte*.
That Winterfeld beast may be a problem. I have no doubt
she'll fill the bidet with roses as her tribute to the dear
deceased designer." He finished, running his hands down
his legs, either checking his creases or adoring himself for
being so chic, so glib.

"I suppose you were upstairs in your room the day
Bruno was murdered," I said.

"Yes. I remember it well."

"Tell me what you remember," I asked, hoping that
he would not complete the Maurice Chevalier moment by
singing.

"I arrived at the house sometime in the morning. I'm
terrible with times. I was here somewhat early, so rather
than wait for a group tour I just started walking around the
place. I wasn't interested in any of the large downstairs
rooms, so I made my way up to the top floor. I looked at all
the rooms. Came downstairs, got in with the groups. Then
we all found poor Megan."

"Did you see anyone upstairs?"

"The police asked me that, so I have thought about
it. The point is I saw everybody. The whole place was
jammed. Except for the spouses it was just about the same
crowd as tonight. Anyone could have walked up the front
stairs, throttled Bruno and tiptoed out the back way."

"What back way?" I asked.

Gus told me that it was a good thing I was a lawyer and not a detective. "When these old houses were built the top floor was for the servants. There was always a narrow back stairway that led directly to the kitchen. It's been screened off for Show House, but it's still there."

"So," I said in sad realization, "each person here had each other for an alibi, but anyone could have done it."

"I'm afraid so. Which still leaves Barry as the *numero uno* suspect," said Gus. He turned toward the door to look at two people who were about to enter the room in close conversation with an older dark-skinned man dressed in full Arabian mufti. They had their arms locked together and were in deep conversation.

"Looks serious," I said.

"I don't know," said Gus. "Maybe it's just another decorative tableau. Two men—chic to sheik."

Not a bad line, I thought as the duo made its way toward us. Bristol was obviously determined to walk by without acknowledging us, so Ally jumped in.

"Nice to see you again, Billy. I thought you'd left for the night."

Bristol kept walking, but his companion stopped them short and looked at us, waiting for an introduction, which Bristol delivered brusquely.

"I'm honored to introduce Dr. Al Zaid."

I stuck out my hand, but the aforementioned introducee put his hands together and bowed my way.

"Welcome to my home," said Dr. Zaid, turning to each of us.

Now I actually was interested. "It is I who am honored, sir. I was under the impression that this home was an embassy or had some governmental connection."

"Yes, I can understand the confusion. I represent a number of Middle East financial groups. We are increasing our investments in your section of the world and I'll be using the home from time to time."

"Do you have any other homes?" asked Ally. Perhaps she was trying to get the worldwide decorating contract.

He may have thought the same thing. He smiled as he answered, "Just a few: Abu Dhabi, Zürich, British Virgin Islands, and now here."

Further conversation was stopped by Bristol, who interjected that he was sure the good Doctor would want to see how the rest of his house had turned out. He gave us a friendly nod and walked out.

"I think I made a mistake with the horse and hounds theme," said Gus. "Arabian knights might have been a better business getter. Do you think he's for real?"

"Could be," I said. "He lives in all the right places. Abu Dhabi, Zürich, and the British Virgins are all financial centers with strict banking secrecy. My guess is that Dr. Zaid moves with very big-time money."

"Very rich," added Gus in a sage tone. "If I'm not mistaken, that was a Pratesi sheet wrapped around his head." This last remark drove Gus into a fit of self-induced laughter. He walked away, waving at us. Ally and I were left standing alone.

"I haven't seen Johnny Bishop," I said, looking around.

"No. Someone said he's still so upset from Megan falling out of the closet and Bruno being murdered that he refused to come to the party."

"Sensitive soul?" I asked.

"It would appear so. He was never that sensitive when we bargained over prices."

"We buy from him?"

"Only for clients. He probably suspects that your budget is more Ben Wa than Renoir."

"Don't knock it. But tell me. Is his stuff legit?"

"It better be. As you might say, people have been killed for less."

"You don't say," I said, looking around and feeling better. "Time to go, Ally. I've had enough cheese puffs to last a lifetime."

She took my arm. "Maybe if you sweet-talk me I'll let you search me for clues."

I smiled. "To the hunt." And we headed for the front door. As we were about to exit, the door opened and there was Stromberg walking in.

"*Que pasa*, Peter?" I asked. "We were just leaving."

"I thought you ought to know," he said. "Someone tried to kill Megan."

"No *merde*, Maigret, what do you think they arrested our client for?" I said, looking at Ally while tipping my hand back in the "he's been drinking too much" sign.

"Gimme a break," said Stromberg. "I mean someone tried to kill her again, today."

"What!" said Ally and I in unison.

"You heard me. This afternoon someone unplugged her life support line. Whoever did it didn't realize that an alarm goes off in the nurses' station if after a minute the patient's breathing on her own. So the alarm goes off, the nurse runs in and plugs her back in, but there's no one else around."

"How's Megan?"

"The same," he answered.

This all must have just happened after I left. "Wow," I said, "where's Barry?"

"Good question," said Stromberg. "The police went to question him and he seems to have disappeared. What should I do?"

"Find him," I said, taking Ally's arm.

"You'll be at home if I need you?" he asked.

"I prefer to think of it as command central, right dear?" I said, looking at Ally.

As we walked away Ally gently whispered in my ear, "Call it whatever you want, just remember who gives the commands." And keeping in step we walked off into the night.

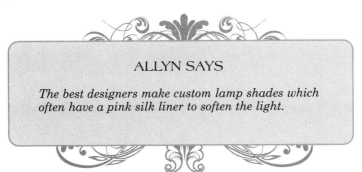

ALLYN SAYS

The best designers make custom lamp shades which often have a pink silk liner to soften the light.

SIXTEEN

At eight o'clock, my morning became electric. The alarm sounded, the automatic coffee machine started grinding the beans, and the phone rang. It was Stromberg to report that there was no sign of Barry. Then the phone rang again, this one was for Ally; and I was able to roll over, hand her the infernal contraption and re-close my eyes. I was still too tired to think clearly. Had it been a night of wanton sex or just "want some sex"? Perhaps too indelicate a question to pose. However, all poses were off when Ally handed me the phone, announcing, "You need the day off. That was Ashworth. The painters are screwing something up in Nantucket and he needs me right away. And I need company."

"I don't know," I responded, "there could be some breaking developments today."

"Bring your cell phone. Who needs you more, me or an accused murderer?"

"The accused murderer."

"Yeah, sure," she said. "But who would you rather...." And here she pressed her face close to mine and whispered sweet somethings into my ear.

"Not fair," I said. At which point she rolled even closer, pressing herself against me, and saying in her deepest pseudo-sexy southern tones, "You know, Porky, you is my man."

"I think that's Porgy, not Porky," I responded.

"Whatever," she replied, languorously pulling the T-shirt in which she had been sleeping over her head.

"On the other hand," I said, slowly moving my other hand. "Maybe you do need me today. Want to know why?"

"Sure thing, honeychile'."

"Because, Breast, you is my woman."

"I think that's Bess," Ally said, as the last bit of clothing dropped away.

"Whatever," I said. But we still made the noon flight from Logan and touched down in Nantucket forty-five minutes later. Who was I kidding, anyway? With a murderer wandering around who might have been my client or anyone else, I wasn't about to let her go by herself.

The island of Nantucket had gone through some remarkable changes since the first colonial canoe landed on its beaches in sixteen-something. It began as a communal sheepherding community, flourished as a whaling port, and ended as a summer home vacation spot. Its name is a Native American term for "faraway island." The last decade had given that name new connotation, as nothing could be farther away from reality than Nantucket. Land values have become the most expensive in the United States. Old homes built by sea captains have been torn down to make room for estates built by captains of finance. Once again, the locals are thriving off big fish; except this time the fish are from Wall Street and Beverly Hills and fly in on private jets to shower their largess on landscapers, contractors, carpenters, painters, and (thanks be to God) decorators.

The compleat angler and I exited the airport to find Steve waiting for us in a red Hummer. The car was certainly *de rigueur* for a guy like Ashworth, who probably assumed that a muscle car, a stunning blond, and a big house covered up his insecurities. He was probably right.

He waved us over and we got in; Ally in the front and me in back. Ashworth was wearing jeans, suitably worn at the knees, a Hilfiger work shirt and a camouflage hat turned backwards so that the brim hung over his ponytail. He looked ready for Desert Storm, but I doubted he was. Unless, of course, it was "Desert Storm—The Movie," and then, with enough special effects, even he had a chance to be a hero.

"Thanks for coming," he began, as we sped out of the airport driveway.

"Our pleasure," said Ally looking pointedly at me to make sure that I would agree if asked. "What's the problem?"

"Between the house and Bunny, it's been a hell of a day."

"Tell me about the house," Ally said.

"Tell me about Bunny," from the backseat drew another pointed look from the front.

"I don't have to tell you," began Ashworth in response, "how important this house is to me. It's more than a place I choose to live in the summer. It's to be a statement of who I am, and how I choose to be seen by the world."

Had this been an airplane I could have derived some comfort from the barf bag in the seat pouch. As it was, I was going to have to restrain myself in every way. I had enough common and monetary sense to keep my gagging to myself.

"Certainly, Steve," Ally said. "That's why we've spent so much time preparing just the right plans and designs for you."

"I feel that Malibu is no longer me. I'm at peace here. The rhythms of the Atlantic Ocean and the simple life. The Pacific is so troubled."

Tell that to Balboa, I thought as we turned off of Cliff Road and onto Washington Circle. This was the highest street in Nantucket, with views out over the harbor and the ocean beyond. Ashworth's simple life was perched on the highest point of the road's cul-de-sac. It probably wasn't more than ten thousand square feet of living space crammed into three stories. Ally told me that Ashworth had paid six million large for the three-quarter-acre lot on which an old summer house had rested for fifty years. He had torn down the old house and was in the process of fashioning his enduring statement to simplicity. We pulled into the circular drive and followed Ashworth through the front door and the entrance hall to the living room.

The first thing that struck me about entering the room was that the back wall was all glass and provided the most spectacular harbor view I'd ever seen in Nantucket. Then I saw the rest of the room. The walls were in the process of being painted. It wasn't quite as sumptuous as the Sistine Chapel, but it was pretty close.

"What are we going to do?" asked Ashworth, who was standing in the living room, feet spread, hands on his hips, as if a modern Colossus of Rhodes guarding the entrance to Nantucket Harbor.

I could see that Ally was at a loss, so I jumped to her aid. "About what, Steve?"

"The moldings, man, the moldings!"

I looked up at the top of the room. I'd been around Ally long enough to know her penchant for crown moldings. Ceilings and walls never just met for my wife. They met and were then enveloped in molding, usually carved and then hand painted. These did look a little off, perhaps because they were red.

"Do you mean the reddish color?" Ally asked in her sweetest voice.

"Yes. Yes," replied Ashford. "I don't want it. I don't like it. Take it away."

Ally had spent years putting up with the tantrums of those with far more money than taste. "Steve," she began, walking over and putting her arm around him, "I wouldn't have done that to you. It's just part of the process. I'm having the wood gilded. They're going to be gold, just the way you wanted. Remember? Beverly Hills sophistication blended with Nantucket charm. But the gilding process starts with red. You'll see. It will be just perfect."

"Oh, thank God," said Ashworth as he walked over and sat on the steps which led to the next level. "You can't believe how relieved I am."

"Is there anything else we can do?" Ally asked, still in her sweetest tones.

"I wish," he said. "This Bunny thing is getting out of hand."

"How so?" I asked.

"She was pretty upset after her father died. The suicide seems to have made her mother so angry that she's been no help. Bunny and I have been hanging out for a while and she seemed to be getting better; but now this Megan thing has driven her 'round the bend again."

"What was Megan to her?" I asked.

"I thought nothing," he responded. "Megan was decorating for Bunny's parents and was around all the time. She even found the body when the old boy killed himself. I guess Bunny was close to her, although I never knew it before."

"Where's Bunny now?" Ally asked.

"Last I saw, she was out back in the garden. C'mon outside, maybe you can cheer her up."

We followed Steve through the sliding door and out to the back lawn which circled the house in a narrow horseshoe shape above the cliff. We could see Bunny sitting on a bench at the side of the property. She seemed to be just staring out over the ocean. Ally and Ashworth went off to talk to her. I stayed back to look around at the grounds. If Bunny had been working out here, she certainly presented an interesting variation on a green thumb. All of the roses had been cut off the bushes; all of the flowers had been shorn from their stems. They lay on the ground where they fell, casting an eerie gothic spell. I looked back for Ally and saw that she and Ashworth were gently prying Bunny's hands off the garden shears that lay in her grasp.

SEVENTEEN

Ally walked Steve and Bunny back into the house, asking if there was anything we could do. Ashworth told us that he had some pills that might help Bunny, and that he'd probably take a few too. He even offered to give us some, which made me wonder if there was actually a physician behind this self-medication. In any event, we declined and decided to walk down to our house and check things out before heading back to Boston. So we strolled off arm in arm down the street and down from the cliff to the area where we and the more common folk lived.

"What do you make of all that?" asked Ally as we walked.

"You mean how once again riche has been wasted on the nouveau and how you and I would be much better at it if we only had the chance?"

"Not that," she said. "The whole Bunny thing."

"Actually, I'm most interested," I said, "because there's a link to Megan, and this link is decapitating flowers."

"You're not suggesting—"

"Like Hercule Poirot, I suggest nothing. I walked out of the MGH yesterday with Steve and Bunny. But apparently they didn't leave right away. Did Bunny go back in and pull Megan's plug, and if she did, why, and what about Bruno?" I said, twisting my nonexistent Belgian mustache. "Eh *mon chérie*, zees are matters for Poirot's leetle gray cells."

"Too bad there's no Poirot, and too few gray cells. Let's get back to the other issue. Can you see what I have to deal with? Don't get me wrong. There are a lot of wonderful clients out there. But some of these jerks spend their work lives surrounded by brainless simpering sycophants and then expect the same mindless devotion from me."

"So what do you do?"

"Grin, bear it, and charge them more. At least some of the fools you represent actually end up in jail. For me there's no end. They sit in gorgeous rooms and keep wondering, 'Is that the right settee? Did I really want those flowers on the end table? Is that ottoman too big?' And, if their lives are so perfect and their heads so empty that they have nothing else to think about, sooner or later they call."

"And then...."

"And then it starts all over again. Which is why I'm so glad I've got you to listen to me and we don't have to rely on drugs to get through the day."

"We don't have to," I said, "but...."

"Forget it," she said. "You went to college. Live on your memories."

And speaking of memories, without even realizing it, we had ambled to our little aerie by the sea. Because I've been so caught up in the design world lately, I think it only fair that I say something about my summer home. When I was a lad and dreamed, not of the British Navy, but a house in Nantucket, I had visions of a rambling old place with a big porch, festooned with Adirondack chairs, hammocks, and old New England people whittling things. The inside would be cozy, with run-down, faux inherited furniture. There would be a stuffed bass or two, a couple of loving cups, and assorted sports memorabilia. All reminders of victories—on the ocean, the golf course, the tennis courts. It would be the kind of house Norman Rockwell could walk into, put up his feet, and read *Boys' Life*.

That dream may have turned into someone's reality but, alas, fate had other plans for me. From the outside it was a typical gray, rose-covered Nantucket cottage. But Mr. Rockwell might never get past my front door. First, he'd have to take off his shoes, so that the dreaded sand would not impact the hand-painted floors. Then his trousers would have to pass inspection before he could sit on the pristine white fabric that was this year's motif. And, lastly, he would have to accept the fact that should he wish to eat or drink, he would receive nothing red (neither sauce nor wine) as that might lead to a stain. Marry a decorator, boys, and you can kiss your bean bags goodbye.

We entered. Everything seemed to be as we had left it before Labor Day. Ally went off to the kitchen and I walked into the den, where I flopped into my favorite easy chair. It was only my favorite because every other piece of furniture was so covered in pillows that simple flopping was an impossibility. What Johnny Appleseed was to his seeds, and young girls are to rosebuds, decorators are to their pillows. Wherever they walk, they scatter pillows in their wake. Sofas and chairs become mere resting places for pouches of silk and goose down. But as I leaned back and looked across the room, I saw something else far more interesting resting on a sofa. In fact, he was more than resting. He was sound asleep, and he was Barry.

I cleared my throat and gave a few vigorous coughs in an attempt to gently rouse Barry. Ally came in, probably to check if I had inhaled a pillow and needed to be given the Heimlich.

"Oh my," she said upon seeing Barry.

"My thoughts exactly. As long as you're here, could you nudge him on the shoulder a bit? We ought to find out what he's doing."

Ally walked over to Barry and gently pushed his shoulder. It worked. Barry sat bolt upright, staring at both of us.

"Sorry to wake you, old boy," I said. "But I was wondering what you are doing sleeping on my couch in Nantucket when a great many people, including my own investigator, are trying to find you."

"Oh Buzz," he said, still sitting on the couch and looking sheepishly at both of us. "When Ally gave me keys to your summer house, and told me to use it if I needed a break, it never occurred to me to call first."

I looked at Ally. "I completely forgot," she said, also looking somewhat sheepish. "I gave Barry the keys after you got him out of jail. I figured we weren't going to be using it much, so—"

"Tell me, Barry," I interjected. "Anything happen that caused you to need a break? Been pushing down any chimneys on my wife, perchance?"

"Oh, Buzz." He crossed his arms and legs nervously. "I may be in a little bit of a mess. I went to see Megan at the hospital yesterday."

"Why?"

"I thought if I could sit with her and pray, maybe she would come to and we could find out who tried to kill her. Anyway, I walked into her room and I immediately knew something was wrong. No sooner had I walked in than a loud buzzer started going off. She was just lying there, a buzzer was buzzing. I stepped back out of the room and I saw a nurse running at me. I guess I panicked and I ran. I went for an exit sign, not even the elevator. I must have run down a million stairs. I got to the bottom, walked out, got in a cab and headed for the airport. I didn't know what to do or where I was going. Then I remembered Ally, and that I had the key on my key ring. I came down last night and I must have spent the whole evening pacing back and forth, crying. I guess I fell asleep on the couch."

"Do you think that the nurse got much of a look at you?"

"I don't know. I just saw her and ran."

"We'll just have to hope for the best. By the way, what do you know about a pretty young thing named Bunny?"

"Rabitsky?"

"Bingo."

"She was hard not to notice. Even for me. When I was in the decorator's building shopping for clients, Megan introduced me to her."

"What was she doing with Megan?"

"I think Megan said she was working for Bunny's parents. Bunny was going along to watch the great one in action. Why?"

"She's popped up with Steve Ashworth, a client of Ally's."

"I met him, too," said Barry. "Bruno and I had dinner with him at Bice in Palm Beach last year. Bruno was trying to hustle some decorating business from him. I understood that he had some bad dealings with Megan— lawsuits were mentioned—and he needed a new designer. I guess you won the beauty contest," he said, turning to Ally.

Here was a guy I was defending for murder, who was hiding out in my house being aided and abetted by my wife, and I couldn't help but detect a note of bitchy resentment in his voice. Apparently, losing a client to Ally took precedence over his current predicament.

"Do you know any details about his problems with Megan?" I asked.

Barry actually turned and started walking out of the room. "Issues, issues, issues," he intoned, waving his arms. "But they weren't my issues, so I paid no attention."

"Well," I responded, "let's get to your issues: you haven't responded to my chimney reference. Have you been at the Show House in the last few days?"

Barry paused at the door. "I knew you'd be mad, so I didn't tell you, but I just had to be there. It's in my blood," he exclaimed. "Unfortunately, or fortunately, I guess, I missed the action."

"Careful," interjected Ally, "Sherlock's about to ask you if anyone saw you not going up on the roof."

Even Barry seemed confused by this interjection. "I'm sorry; I just went over and wandered around. By the way," he said looking over at Ally, "I just love that green rug."

"Do you really?" she responded. "I was worried about some of the beiges."

"Oh, don't be silly," Barry started to say, but before he finished I jumped up.

"Enough!" I yelled. "We are going back to Boston. Ally, let's take a stroll into town and grab a cab to the airport. Other than catching my own client before he becomes a full-fledged fugitive, this has been a major waste of time."

Downcast, with his hands stuffed in his pockets, Barry walked out of our house and towards the sidewalk. After I locked up, we followed.

"Maybe not such a waste of time," said Ally. "People are starting to get strangely linked with Megan. Maybe we have some suspects."

"You know what I suspect?" I asked as we started walking down the path.

"No."

"Well, with all this commotion I never really had a chance to ponder on the sartorial elegance of our friend here," and saying this I pointed to Barry who was walking ahead of us. He was wearing lime green pants and a multicolored sweater over a pink turtleneck collar. On his head was a beret that matched his pants. "So what I suspect is that the nurse saw him, and, assuming that, I wonder if anyone saw him on the roof?"

"Don't be ridiculous. He couldn't hurt anyone. We've been friends for years."

Said the serial killer's longtime neighbor, I thought, as we caught up with Barry. The three of us walked to town, cabbed to the airport, and Ally and I were in bed by ten.

EIGHTEEN

The next day started well. I explained to the police that Barry was with us in Nantucket. Apparently, the nurse hadn't noticed Barry, which goes a long way toward explaining how they can leave scalpels inside of surgery patients. All was clear on that score, which was a good thing as I needed to put aside distractions and get back to my regular practice of law, not to mention my regular life.

The new post-summer year, which had only recently dawned, was under way. The days of September hurried into autumn. Our lives had become routine for another year. Ally was busy with clients and Show House. Justin was moving well through the eighth grade, dividing his time between studies, friends, sports, and computers. Fortunately, he still needed me for rides to school and help with Latin, so I wasn't completely out of his loop. Maria was taking cooking classes. The results would have been better if she had also taken English classes. She did well with numbers, so the measurements and timing were flawless. However, her inability to distinguish between the words for an animal's ass and its elbow led to several gastronomic surprises.

I was lawyering up a storm. Mrs. Hirsch was happy because I succeeded in tying up all of her husband's assets.

In an incredible stroke of luck, the constable arrived at Hirsch's bank with a restraining order only minutes before a wire transfer was about to shift various millions to Switzerland and Panama. We had also blocked Hirsch's access to any of his safe deposit boxes. He was talking about reconciliation. Mrs. Hirsch, a strict devotee of the twenty-four-karat golden rule, was interested if the price was right.

I never did get to see Gina Williams again. The victory over Professor Goodman was a quick TKO. The judge read our brief, threw out the case, and ordered Goodman to pay all costs. His Honor also strongly suggested that Goodman undergo psychiatric counseling. When last heard from, the Professor was threatening to sue the judge.

The firm was moving ahead like a well-oiled machine. I continued to schedule depositions and appointments at times that were guaranteed to conflict with partners' meetings. Were it not for the slight problem of Barry's trial, all would have been perfect. The trial wasn't scheduled until sometime after the first of the year, but I was clearing my decks and dockets in order to devote myself full time to this case. For her part, Megan was still sound asleep, as if cursed by some wicked queen. Which, come to think of it, was pretty close to what the police were claiming.

On a beautiful fall morning, I sat in my office looking out over the harbor. There were still a few sailboats at their moorings. The sun reflected low over the water. My feet were up on my desk as I sat back, my mind lost in thought: the meaning of life, the future of law, secondary uses of flanken, that sort of thing. More fruitful daydreaming centered on the ski season that would be arriving soon.

We were a skiing family, a cohesive schussing unit made up of distinct styles. Justin had been skiing since early youth. He was good. Truth be told, I was as good at this particular sport as I was at all others—not very.

However, enthusiasm could cover a multitude of missteps, and as long as my insurance was paid there was no keeping me from the black diamonds. Ally had a totally different approach to the sport. She liked the look, which was mostly haute couture Bogner, and the feel, particularly of places like Little Nell. It was the snow that didn't thrill her too much. So most winter vacations we'd try to head for Aspen where, after an exhilarating day, Justin and I could regale Ally with tales of trails like Ruthie's Run, and she could return the favor with tales of sales at Revillon. Ah, wilderness.

So when you put all these daydreams together, was everything hunky-dory? You know something? I think so. Every case can be planned out with a theory of the case, but can you direct yourself with a theory of life? I don't think so. Hope to be loved, hope to love, keep your health—all the rest is commentary.

Stromberg entered the room and I assumed an upright position, ready to work. "Peter," I said. "It's time to get focused. I think the only focus we have is Claridge, although there are some strange coincidences from the Ashworth-Rabitsky camp. I've still got to catch up with Bishop. He may be a nice surprise."

"You think there's something fishy in all the financial stuff I found?"

"Absolutely. Plus, Billy Bristol is definitely not on the level. Even for a decorator. I'm going to go over to Claridge and see if I can stir up the pot a little. I'd like you to go to New York. Claridge's headquarters are in the design center. I have no idea what we're looking for so let's do a little fishing. Maybe we'll actually catch something. Get some expense money from the bookkeeper and we'll talk in a few days."

My faithful shamus rose and headed for the door. "To the hunt, boss." Maybe Gus was on to something.

I saw him out, returned a few phone calls, and struck out for Claridge's store, hoping I wouldn't *actually* strike out.

NINETEEN

The Boston Design Center is located on the waterfront in the old Naval Base. The Navy had abandoned Boston years ago, and some of the old buildings were redesigned as part of an urban renewal scheme. The Center is a long, sprawling building now totally given over to showrooms and sales offices for decorator furnishings. This place had become the ultimate example of what could happen when swords were turned into plowshares. Scuds had become sconces, bombs had become bureaus, and Naval Jelly, from the looks of the crowd, had been replaced with K-Y jelly.

I parked in the lot and walked off toward the building. There were several people along the way either entering or leaving and they all had that telltale decorator look. The key is that they carry bags of fabrics and samples. The building was only open to the trade, so the idea was that decorators shopped the various showrooms, bringing swatches and samples to their clients. The clients looked over the results of these labors, hopefully oohed and aahed at the most expensive items, and sent their decorators back to the building to order up a storm. I had been to enough functions with Ally to be able to vaguely recognize most of the people along the way. We nodded as we passed.

As I watched some of them, bags and notebooks in hand, heads down, purposefully striding toward the showrooms, I had the feeling that there was still something military in the air. These were seasoned troops, used to fighting on two fronts—for their clients and with their clients. Some were able to take the stress of the fights better than others. Some, like the two women just ahead, were as vicious as any commando, but as insecure as a commando dropped behind enemy lines.

"Good morning, ladies." I tipped my nonexistent hat with insincere civility.

"Hello, Buzz. Don't tell me you've given up law to work for your wife."

"You're not afraid of a little more competition, are you?" I responded. Actually, I knew that's just what they were afraid of. Gwen Rogers, the utterer, and her partner, Mary Lawrence, were known piranhas. When they weren't bad-mouthing each other, they had nothing nice to say about anyone else, either. They took it as a personal insult when any other decorator got a job. Rumor had it that whenever someone in Boston got published in a national decorating magazine, they went into periods of mourning. Obviously, today they were out of mourning. Gwen was dressed all in orange, but it was fall so maybe this was her pumpkin motif.

We walked together in silence until we reached the front desk. I signed in and took the elevator to Claridge's office on the second floor. Claridge appeared to have the largest showroom in the Center. Entrance was gained by walking down a hall past rows of Claridge windows holding displays of hanging fabrics and wallpapers. Even a Philistine like me would have to admit that the stuff was beautiful. While it would have been easier to imagine a murderer lurking in the aisles of an adult bookstore than lounging on a Louis XIV bergère, I was prepared to take my villain where I found him. I went in.

A remarkably preppy young woman, straight from the pages of a Ralph Lauren catalog, greeted me at the front desk. Again my senses were disoriented. If you've read as much Mickey Spillane as I have, you know that front desks are peopled by tough broads in tight dresses who stand in their spike heels whenever Mike Hammer approaches and utter some appropriately smutty double entendre. I couldn't imagine even a single entendre from this pretty young thing.

"Good morning," she said. "How can I be of service to you?" She winked. So much for preconceived dress code bias.

I asked if Billy Bristol was around and she told me that I could wander until I found him. I found him on the telephone at a desk midway through the studio. He looked up as I approached and held up a hand to indicate that I should wait. I drifted about, looking at rows of hanging fabrics. I was used to rows of filing cabinets, but here the aisles were placed between high metal racks from which the Claridge wares were hanging. I recognized some as the materials that appeared in my own home. Bristol seemed deeply involved in his phone conversation, so I kept roaming. With nothing better to do, I decided to play detective and look for a sample of the cloth that was wrapped around Megan's head. I couldn't find it and was running out of things to do when Bristol got off the phone and called me over.

"Sorry to keep you waiting, Mr. Levin."

"No problem. I've always wanted to decorate something myself, so I was just looking at the fabrics, planning renovations for my summer house."

He smirked. "Even if I thought you were serious, you're a tad late. Our new line is about to be displayed and I'm afraid most of what you've looked at will be discontinued."

"I'll stick to law. Speaking of which, I wonder if you can give me some help with my defense of Barry."

"Fire away."

"I suppose Bruno, Megan, and Barry were all customers and friends of yours."

"Certainly customers," he said. "I never really counted any of them my friends."

We walked around the showroom as we spoke and came to a row of fabrics that, even to my untutored eyes, looked dramatically different from the usual Claridge products. These had a very bright Mexican or Latin look. I stopped in front of them. "I imagine the loss of Megan and Bruno will cause a drop in your orders for a while."

"Oh, I don't think so," he replied. "Megan really didn't have much business. And I'd say that Bruno was just an average customer."

Given Stromberg's financial report, it was clear that Bristol was lying. Fortunately for civilization, not all liars are also murderers. But here was an opening that demanded further work at a later date. I changed subjects. "These fabrics look very different from the rest of the showroom."

"I'm rather proud of them," Billy said. "So many wealthy Latin Americans are settling here that I decided to put in a line of Latin goods. They're doing very well." He walked on rapidly toward several people who appeared to be waiting for him. He stopped, spoke briefly, and signed a number of documents.

We had reached the back of the showroom. Next to me was a door with a small glass window. I looked in and it appeared that this was the shipping department. While Bristol was engaged, I decided to nose around a bit. I opened the door and stepped in. Two men were busy rolling up long bolts of fabric around tubes for mailing. We received so many of Ally's orders at home that I was quite familiar with the finished product.

Bristol came through the door and hurriedly walked over to me. "Ah, I see you've found the shipping department. Shall we go out to the main floor and leave these men to their work?" He took my arm to guide me out and I got the distinct impression that I was unwelcome.

"In any event, getting back to Barry, were you aware of any business connection between Megan and Bruno?"

"No."

"Any personal connection?"

"No."

For the next fifteen minutes, I asked every question I could think of that had any relationship to the case. In each instance, Bristol responded in the negative. No query was too insignificant for denial.

"So tell me, what's with that Arabian fellow I saw you with the other night?" I asked.

"Oh, just someone with a great deal of money whose business I'd like to get."

"Gee," I said with as little guile as possible. "You two seemed friendly. Do you know much about him?"

"No."

"What's his business?"

"I really couldn't say. Mutual friends introduced us in Gstaad last season." Bristol seemed sincere and even pronounced Gstaad with the suitably silent G, indicating that he may actually have been there; even so, I still pictured him more with the G-string than the Gstaad crowd. We bantered a bit longer. He grew impatient and I grew weary as we walked toward the front desk. By the time we arrived at the end of our pointless promenade, I'd had enough. I thanked Bristol, winked at the receptionist and headed for the exit.

To sum up, I learned only that Bristol didn't want to tell me anything. I traveled back to the office. Maybe Stromberg had some news.

A TIP FROM ALLYN

Gros point fabrics can be bound and used as rugs in rooms with low traffic. This creates a needlepoint rug effect at a fraction of the price of the real thing.

TWENTY

Barry was waiting for me at the office, which turned out to be a blessing. When I got there, a partners' meeting was about to commence on whether or not we should hire a full-time messenger. This was so critical an issue that Jack had prepared a multi-page position paper on the subject. He had graphs, charts and statistical analysis documenting the number of deliveries we did in an average week, the cost of delivery services, and the benefits and detriments of adding the overhead of our own employee to do deliveries. In one section of his report, I saw a discussion of the possible use of individuals on early prison release programs. With great insight, Jack pointed out that, although we would have to pay less than minimum wage, there was some concern about the fate of our deliveries. I needed an excuse and Barry was it. Stromberg got there shortly after I did and we all repaired to my office.

I sat behind my desk. Barry and Peter took seats in front of me. Barry looked like he was ready for hard work. He was dressed in a purple Calvin Klein workout suit and Reebok cross-trainers, as if he anticipated some heavy lifting. It occurred to me that perhaps he anticipated more from the cross trainers than Reebok did when they chose that particular style name. He sat in colorful contrast to

Stromberg, who was bedecked in a rayon blazer and indecipherable trousers. No cross-trainers for Stromberg; he was solidly anchored to the floor in manly Cordovan wingtips.

I filled them in on my morning. "So, fellows," I said, "Let's look at what we've got. Bruno and Megan were somehow linked together. The evidence points to a sex link, but we should not disregard a business possibility—remember, Megan came in to cover Bruno's bad check at Farcus's. As to Bruno, we've learned that something very strange was going on with his business. Millions of dollars were flowing through the account, but Barry has found very little that stuck. The money trail points us in the direction of Claridge. There we discover Mr. Bristol, who lies about his connection to Bruno and can't wait to get rid of me. Assuming that there's nothing personal in Bristol's attitude towards me, could this be a lead?"

"As requested," Stromberg added, "I spent the morning at Claridge's store in New York. Everyone was happy to talk about Bristol. He's the fair-haired boy of the organization. Boston was a very average market until Bristol got this idea to sell fabric and wallpaper from Latin America. Now sales of this new stuff are booming and Bristol's a hero."

"The whole thing strikes me as most peculiar," said Barry.

"I went back and looked through our records. I saw all of the bank deposits and I saw all of the checks written out to Claridge. There's no profit. Just about every cent that came in went out."

"Maybe Bristol and Bruno were cheating you and Claridge," I suggested.

"I thought so," Barry continued. "But all of the checks were deposited to Claridge."

"No problem so far."

"Except, when I looked closer at the check I could

see the stamp 'Deposit to the Account of Claridge and Sons, Citibank.'"

"So?" said Stromberg

"Citibank B.V.I.," said Barry. "Isn't that a bit unusual? I looked at some of the checks that went to Claridge on fabric that I ordered and those were deposited in Citibank, New York. The account numbers were different."

We all sat looking at each other, the wheels of our internal calculators spinning away. In the midst of the spinning, the door opened and Ally and Justin entered.

"Hi, boys," she said. "Any breaking news?"

I introduced Justin to my guests, and he and Ally took seats on the window sill.

"What brings my entire family into town?" I asked.

"It was advisor day and Justin got out early. In exchange for four times the minimum wage he agreed to help me run some errands in town. We were nearby and thought we'd look in on the man who pays the bills. What's new?"

I summed up the previous discussion for Ally and Justin. "Any thoughts?"

"You know, Dad," said the light of my life. "If you spent more time watching TV, and less time reading great books, you'd have cracked this case a long time ago."

"Okay, Columbo—fill us in."

"Not Columbo, Dad, wrong reruns, try *CSI: Miami*. Look what you got here, lots of money going to a bank in the Caribbean and guys selling stuff from Latin America. And where in Latin America, might I ask?"

I hated that supercilious tone, but the kid was going in the right direction. "I believe Colombia was mentioned."

"Colombia? Hmm, what do they make again? Hello? Discovery Channel?"

"Well I'll be," I said. "I think he's got it."

"See Buzz, I told you cable would pay for itself. Come along, Justin," said Ally, rising to leave. "Our work is done here. Let's ride off into the sunset." Justin gave her a look which only proved that he might know a lot about vice and drugs in Miami, but he knew nothing of the Lone Ranger. "Call us when you need us again." And they left.

When they were gone, the room was as quiet as when they'd come in. Stromberg broke the silence. "That was my hunch, too."

"Oh, yeah. Some detective. At least you're cheaper than the kid. But it does seem, Barry, that your partner had moved from decorator to dealer."

Barry stood and walked to the window. Looking out over the harbor, he placed both palms against the window, leaning forward as if he were dreaming of flight. Away from this room, away from his troubles. After a moment he turned toward us. "I've known nothing. My love, my respectability, and my life were all stolen from me. Who am I now?"

"Barry," I said. "Don't think me insensitive, but an existential dilemma will have to wait another day. We have a trial coming up. Fast."

Stromberg was even less sensitive than I as he appeared to miss the entire conversation. "Obviously the drugs were packed in the fabrics. The coke could be stuffed into the middle of the cardboard tube and shipped directly into Claridge for reshipment."

"Bristol must have been in charge of distribution and Bruno handled sales," I continued. "He washed the money through his account on its way to a Caribbean bank. Anyone looking at the checks would see that they were made out to Claridge. It just wasn't the same Claridge. Any hope of getting information from that Virgin Islands bank?"

"None," said Stromberg. "When the Swiss got easy, places like the Virgin Islands and Abu Dhabi got tough. It's a bagman's paradise."

"Well, this certainly is a day of remarkable coincidences." I said. "For years I hadn't heard anyone mention Abu Dhabi, and suddenly it just keeps popping up all over the place. Let's do some more fishing. Not every drug dealer is a murderer. We need connections. Did Megan, Bruno, or Bristol travel to the Virgin Islands? Did Megan make out any checks to the phony Claridge account? And, of course, what went wrong in paradise? Of the three, shall we say, 'importers,' only Bristol is left. Why? And last but not least, to add a touch of romance, where does the sheik from Show House fit into all of this?"

My client and investigator walked out of the room, one nodding resolutely, understanding the task ahead, the other as confused as ever. And I, the rakish combination of Perry Mason and Nick Charles, waited for the door to close before putting my feet up and aiming my chair out over the harbor. I had almost gotten through the first verse of "Sittin' on the Dock of the Bay" when the door opened and Lisa came in to ruin what was left of the day with the arrival of another lawyer's dilemma—a potential client. Truly a mixed blessing. The good news was that one's services were still in demand. The bad news was that perhaps I was going to have to do something. Which reminded me; I had something to do tomorrow. Show House was opening to the public, and I thought a return to the scene of the crime was in order. The dock, the bay, and the sittin' would have to wait. There were clients to see, murders to solve, and wives to protect.

Especially wives to protect.

ALLYN RECOMMENDS

Perfume on light bulbs provides a nice aroma for a room.

TWENTY-ONE

When I awoke the next morning, Ally was already dressed and standing in front of the bedroom mirror, adjusting her earrings.

"Did I oversleep?" I asked.

"Nope, but you under-remembered. Today's the opening of Show House. I've got to get there early to make sure that my room is clean and the flowers are fresh. Then I'm there for the day. This year they're having all the designers stand in their rooms for the opening."

"So you can be there for the oohing and ahhing of the unwashed masses?"

"I had my sights set on the upper classes. But I'll take my oohs and ahhs where I get them."

"Come a little closer," I said propping myself up on an elbow, "and I'll let you stick out your tongue and say aaah."

"And then I suppose you'll supply the tongue depressor," she said as she walked toward the door, "Sorry, today I'm playing decorator, not doctor."

"That's okay, we could play the lucky client and the naughty decorator game."

"Gotta run. You'll have to fluff up your own pillows." She turned at the door. "Will I see you there?"

"Have I ever missed an opening?" I said as she blew me a kiss and walked out the door.

And I certainly wasn't going to miss this one. It was, after all, the scene of the crime, and who knew who would be returning to it. Let Ally get her oohs, I still held out hope for clues. There was also the minor matter of keeping the little woman alive and kicking—or at least alive.

Justin was finishing breakfast when I made my tardy arrival in the breakfast room. As I walked in he walked out with a quick wave. A kid down the street who went to school with Justin had recently gotten his license and had become the designated neighborhood driver. Time was passing and I was beginning to feel phased out. But these were thoughts for another day as I tightened my tie and headed for town.

When I arrived at Beacon Hill, there was already a line at the front door of the Show House. The way these things work is that the public queues up to buy tickets at the front door. Once inside, they are given a book that lists the rooms, contains a brief statement about each room by the designer, and lists the vendors and suppliers used by each decorator. It's great advertising for all, so suppliers usually give the designers substantial discounts in exchange for inclusion in the list. On opening day, many of the vendors and workrooms send representatives to answer questions.

After receiving their books, the visitors are directed by ever-so-polite, smiling and refined Leaguers (none of whom would be caught dead inviting these people into their real homes) along the path that would bring them to each room in proper order. The idea was to get them in the front and out the back, where a tent had been erected to house a gift shop and coffee bar.

Since I already knew the drill, I walked quickly around the line of people without bothering to look at the rooms. I did pass close enough to confirm that there actually were oohs and ahhs. There were also a few yechs, but none, I'm pleased to report, in front of the room of my beloved. I arrived at her room and stepped inside next to her.

"How's it going?" I asked.

"My feet are killing me," she said *sotto voce* as she smiled at the people passing by.

"In this house you're lucky that's all that's killing you. Speaking of which, I'm on the lookout for a couple of characters who were there when you found Megan. Johnny Bishop and the drapery fellow, Frankie."

"They're walking around together somewhere. Try the coffee bar out back."

"Together? Then it's true."

"What?"

"Frankie and Johnny are lovers."

Ally kept smiling at the people looking in the room as she elbowed me. "Keep that up and I'll put the hounds on you."

I looked over at the stone dogs I had once been conscripted to schlep and, murmuring "Not the hounds, m'lady," made my way out of the room. She pulled at my arm before I left. "If you see Frankie, be nice to him. His workroom did Ashworth's California house, and I may have to use him again."

"I'm nice to everybody," I said, leaving the room, smiling graciously at women who were looking in, pointing, and yes, oohing and ahhing. I walked down the back stairs looking for the exit. I envisioned someone else walking down these same stairs. He or she had just come from murdering Bruno. I slowed my step, trying to take in whatever psychic vibrations were in the air, hoping that Mr. or Ms. X would be revealed. Nothing. Nothing, that is, until I received a poke in the back, almost causing me to lose my step.

"Hurry up, young man." I turned to see the speaker and poker. She was old enough to be a Confederate War widow, and was brandishing her cane like a saber. They were a tough crowd, these Beacon Hill decorator devotees, and I wasn't going to mess with this one. I picked up my pace and made it out the back door with neither a psychic in sight nor cane in back.

Arriving at the back of the house, I came upon a patio surrounded by gardens, all covered by a large green and white striped tent, under which were several tables and chairs. There was an espresso/coffee/latte bar in one corner of the tent, and along another side were laid out long tables with gift items. I entered and surveyed the scene. Most of the tables were occupied by groups of older women who were, based upon their style of dress (a style which could not be acquired, only inherited), obviously Leaguers in their day. It was interesting to see them sip coffee and nibble scones. Although this group could speak with a closed mouth, the act of eating actually required jaw movement. Apparently their evolution was not complete.

Off to the side there was a table that held even more interest. Two younger men were sitting in conversation with what appeared to be a male biker and his female counterpart. The guy was dressed in black leathers and his head was completely shaved. He had a nose ring that was connected by a silver chain to a lip ring. The girl had hair—bright orange and spiked upward. She, too, had lip rings, one on either side of her mouth. These had thin chains which were connected to the rings and dropped down into her jersey. A clue to their ultimate connection was that when she opened and closed her mouth, her chest seemed to rise and fall. Perhaps she was pledging the League. I'd find out soon enough. The men were Johnny and Frankie.

I grabbed a cup of coffee and, in my best aimless manner, walked over to their table.

"Mind if I sit down?"

"We'd be honored," said Johnny. Turning to Frankie he added, "This is Buzz Levin. He's representing Barry."

"Oh," said Frankie. The bikers grunted. I sat down.

Johnny was dressed in sharp contrast to the bikers. He looked like an art dealer was probably supposed to look: pressed brown pants, tweed jacket, knit tie. Frankie probably looked like a drapery maker was supposed to look: skin tight jeans, tight woven polo shirt, and a silver bracelet on each wrist.

Frankie shook my hand, and pointed to the other two at the table. "These are my very talented assistants, Bruce and Rebecca."

Probably noticing my lifted eyebrows when their names were announced, Bruce grunted back at Frankie, "Hey, that's Scum and Skank."

Frankie looked at me with a mock smile. "How could I have forgotten? This week they're in their retro punk mode. It seems like only yesterday I was at their wedding, Bruce and Rebecca Glassfogel."

"Watch it," said the girl, ending with a grimace so exaggerated that it caused her breasts to rise up and point at Frankie. As fun as this palaver was, I had to get down to business. I turned to my prey.

"So, how does it feel coming back to this house? I understand you were both here when the bodies were discovered."

"A day I'll never forget," said Johnny. "My paintings are all over the walls and I wanted at least one look."

"Same for my drapes," said Frankie. "I keep wondering why Barry did it."

"Maybe he didn't," I said.

"Who else would have wanted to kill both of them?" Johnny asked. "Personally I never liked Bruno, but I hardly knew Megan."

"Why the dislike?"

"He was always looking to chisel on prices. Fancied himself a big businessman with all the angles. But don't get me wrong, I wouldn't kill him."

"Did you do much business with him?" I asked.

"Hardly any. You knew them better than I," said Johnny, turning to Frankie.

"Hey," said Frankie. "Please don't get me involved. I know nothing. Sure, I used to see them around together all the time. But let me repeat: I know nothing."

"Yeah," said Rebecca/Skank. "Who could know anything about them? What a couple of dips. Frankie, Scum and me saw them at a club just before it happened. Remember, they were all tight, only talking to each other, whispering for like hours, man."

"Assholes. Pointed at me and laughed. Should have fucking done them then," muttered Scum, who then looked around and added, "But it wasn't me."

"That's 'I,' Bruce," I said for some reason that could only be caused by my subconscious empathy for Bruce's parents.

"Either way's right, and it's Scum, asshole."

The pot was getting stirred quite nicely and I had high hopes for an insightful encounter, when my tablemates grew strangely silent, all looking over my shoulder.

I saw their looks and turned around. The cause of all this quietude was standing behind me. I stood up, turning around, and was face to face with a sheepish Barry.

"What are you doing here?" I asked, taking his elbow and pulling him aside.

"Don't be mad, Buzz. I just couldn't sit around anymore with nothing to do. I've always loved Show House, and so many of my friends are here I simply had to come to the opening."

I looked around. Most of the people in the room were nodding, whispering and pointing our way. I glanced back at my table where Frankie, Johnny and friends were gathering up their belongings, uttering a few "see you later's" and heading for the hills. As they left, most of the people turned to stare at the unusual entourage, and I used the opportunity to push Barry down into a seat.

"I suppose you know you interrupted a great little interrogation I had going on here."

"Really? Sorry.... So, tell me. What do you think? Maybe that awful Bruce did it?"

"He looks the part, but I think that beneath all that punk, there's still a Glassfogel waiting to get out. You're probably right about Frankie. Whatever the murdering type is, he doesn't strike me as it. I would have liked to have spent more time with Johnny."

I could tell he was going to apologize again, so I kept going. "Have some coffee and let's get out of here. I don't want to see headlines or even articles in the society page about how you returned to the scene of the crime. We're going to walk out of here, and I want you to smile at all the good people as we go. And then go home, and wait for further instructions."

"What instructions?"

"The ones where I tell you to stay home. No more trips to Nantucket. Not to the Show House. Not even to the outhouse. Get it?"

"Got it."

"Good!" And so saying, we began to make our exit stage right, through the assembled Leaguers looking our way, chased not by a bear, but a stare. That is, until we heard the crash, followed by yelling and, of all people, Ashworth, telling me there was an accident in Ally's room.

TWENTY-TWO

Ashworth's announcement was like the sounding of a starter's gun at a 100-yard dash. I took off, running out of the tent, into the house, and around toward Ally's room. There was a crowd at the door and I pushed through, hoping for the best.

Were it not for the crash and the screaming, the scene in the room would have been ambiguous at best. A man was on the floor, flat on his back. Ally was on her knees next to him. She was just pushing her hair back out of her face and leaning over him when I yelled, "Hey!"

"Quiet," she said. "It's been a long time since I've done this. I've got to concentrate."

And, to my relief, she began to give mouth-to-mouth resuscitation to the man on the floor. I walked over and saw that it was Gus. Except for one small matter, he looked pretty good: velvet jump suit with matching cape spread out beneath him. He could have been an old Gainsborough boy taking a nap. His X-rated walking stick lay nearby. The small matter, of course, was that he wasn't breathing. I also detected the smell of burnt flesh.

Obviously, Ally had once received a merit badge in resuscitation. Her huffs and puffs were rewarded by movement in Gus' limbs. He began to stir. He slowly opened his eyes to see Ally's lips locked on his, whereupon he screamed, sat up straight (pushing Ally over onto the floor) and fainted dead away—but at least not completely dead.

I offered Ally my hand and she bounded up.

"What happened?" I asked.

"One of the lights in the chandelier was flickering. I couldn't reach the bulb, so I called in Gus from the next room. He pulled over an ottoman and stood on it to reach the light. As soon as he touched the bulb, there was a loud bang, sparks shot out, and he was knocked off the chair. I figured it was an electric shock. Lucky for him I took lifesaving in junior high."

"Junior high? Lucky for him you took ginkgo biloba this morning."

I saw the crowd at the door move apart as two EMTs came in wheeling a stretcher. Gus was just coming to when they loaded him onto the gurney. I explained the injury to them as they took him out. "Go easy," I admonished. "He's just had two shocks."

When the room cleared, I pulled over a chair and stood on it to examine the chandelier. One of the lights was burned out. There were wires coming out of the socket running up alongside the bulb. The jolt Gus got was no accident. This had been designed to shock anyone who tried to fix the light, and it was clear that "anyone" was supposed to be Ally. If Gus hadn't been around to help, she'd be the one on the stretcher and without the benefit of resuscitation. Blind luck had saved her again, but luck's not a very reliable bodyguard. Granted, *I* wasn't much of a bodyguard, but at least I was reliable and I wasn't going anywhere. Remember my lack of a purpose in life? Well, now I had one: Save Ally.

"Who has been around here today?"

"Everyone," she answered. "I even saw Barry. I thought you told him to stay home. What was he doing here?"

"Good question. He's becoming a usual suspect. Which is not a pleasant thought. We'll have to see how this plays out. In the meantime, I think we'll spend the day together."

"Buzz, I can't leave the room today."

"Not to worry, I'll be by your side. Worrying about you would ruin the day. So I might as well ruin it in this decorative splendor, where I can make sure you're safe."

And so I stood by my woman for the rest of the day. As predicted, she got many oohs and ahhs. I garnered only an occasional eh, but it was a day well spent. That night we agreed that, decoratively speaking, it was a great opening. And, as there was clearly more to life than a well-received room, we also agreed that until this case was solved, over-protectiveness would not be viewed as neurotic, but as the watchword of our faith.

TWENTY-THREE

I'm sure there's a common perception that lawyers only have one case at a time. Perry Mason only had one murder a week, and no other clients. But real life is different. Few lawyers are secure enough to close their doors and turn off their phones on behalf of any client. This creates the impossible task of giving each client one hundred percent of your energy, while still accepting new cases, trying to solve new problems, and even paying the rent.

So in the midst of pondering my next step in the cause de Barry, real life appeared in the form of Lisa, announcing that I had a visitor. She'd never seen the fellow before, but apparently he knew all about me and, according to Lisa, was here to hire me. I'd never had a good experience with people who walked in off the street. This, too, is contrary to popular TV impression. Still, I instructed her to bring him in.

As a young lawyer, I believed that my big break would come as it had to Paul Newman in *The Young Philadelphians*. An old lady would come to the office and be ignored by all of the busy senior partners—only I would have time for her. She would be a dowager empress and my future would be set. Actually, years ago something like that happened. The only difference was that my little old lady had lost all of her money in bad investments and came to me to sue the International Communist Conspiracy who had taken all of her cash as part of their diabolical plot to expand their evil empire. I was sad to turn down her case and even sadder to find out that she had complained to the Board of Bar Overseers that I was in league with unnamed Communists. My sadness reached its apogee when I received a communication from the Bar informing me that they treated all complaints seriously and I was forced to return a detailed rebuttal. All in all, I learned that both little old ladies off the street and the Board of Bar Overseers often have difficulty discerning fact from fiction.

The following years produced several more walk-ins. They all had definite needs, but none were as legal as they had hoped. One man needed an injunction to keep the CIA from following him. Another wanted to sue the Atomic Energy Commission for controlling his brainwaves. Sellers of suits with two pairs of pants might thrive on dragging in customers who were walking by, but not lawyers. So I was prepared for another short and bizarre meeting.

Lisa reopened the door and showed in Mr. Sol Finebloom. And, if you will allow me to digress from the story in chief, it was a meeting that was to begin one of my most memorable representations. To all the world, and me in particular, Mr. Finebloom must have appeared to be a nice little old man. Appearances can be deceptive. I once ate breakfast in Miami and had a pleasant chat with the nice little old man sitting next to me who was later revealed to be Meyer Lansky. Since then, I've made it a practice to reserve judgment about individuals with Mr. Finebloom's mien until after I get to know them.

I visually scanned Finebloom, looking for telltale signs of dementia. He was probably seventy-five years old, 5' 6" or so, with wispy white hair and a pleasant smile. He wore a well-tailored suit, white shirt and metallic blue tie much favored by the AARP set, whose wives often have matching hair.

I offered Mr. Finebloom a seat, and he handed me his business card, which bore the following: a very small picture of a smiling fish beneath "Fine Herring," and below the fish, "Solomon Finebloom, President."

"Perhaps you've heard of us?" he queried softly.

"I've more than heard," I exclaimed with unconcealed enthusiasm. "I'm a great fan of your products. Prepared foods are a way of life in my house, and I think I was munching on some of your matjes just the other night."

To this, Mr. Finebloom gave a serious nod of approval. "I was right to come here. Herring has been my life and now that son of a bitch Kravitzky is out to steal my life."

"Kravitsky?"

"Kravitco. Salty crackers, plain crackers, you know—very big in crackers."

"Sure," I responded. "I think that's what I had your herring on the other night. They go well together."

A look of despair crossed Finebloom's face. "That, boychick, is the problem."

As I was about to speak he held up his hand. "First, some history.

"In 1904 my father, Isadore Finebloom, and his best friend Isadore Kravitsky decided that being drafted into the Czar's army was not what they had in mind for life. So one cool fall morning they said goodbye to native Kiev and headed west. After about a year and a half they ended up in the lower east side of New York. There the two Izzy's, as they were known, set out to hustle their way to the top.

"My father got a job with a herring peddler, Kravitsky with a baker. In a couple of years, they each had their own place. Then a few places. Then a chain of places. Then factories, trucks, executive offices—the whole megillah. Along the way, they each got married, had families, moved to Queens, then Great Neck. I never went to college. I left high school in the depression and went right into herring. I salted them, I pickled them, I smoked and I kippered. Regrets, I have none. In 1978, we went public, and my family and I control thirty-seven percent of the stock.

"Kravitsky also had a son. Marcus. What a name. From the day he was born they thought he was going to be a Roman emperor. We were semi-friends as kids, but when I went into herring and he went on to Harvard we drifted apart. I got sick listening to his mother. 'My Marcus, what a genius. Someday he'll be president.' Harvard did wonders for Marcus. By the time he'd finished with college and then business school, he had learned how to go out with blond society girls, drink bourbon instead of slivovitz, and change his name. He thought Kravess had more class than Kravitsky."

"Marcus Kravess? The leverage buyout king?"

"The very same. He got his MBA, returned home and convinced his father to give him the business. Shortly after which his mother and father ended up in West Palm Beach, never to be heard from or visited again. So, as anyone who reads the *Journal* knows, Kravess hyped the stock and went public. Then he used the company's assets and very junky bonds to take over a cosmetics company, a bank, and lots more. Not to forget is the fact that he's a ruthless mamzer who's screwed everyone who ever dealt with him. Now he wants my herring."

"Why herring?" I said, intrigued.

"Why indeed," Finebloom responded. "His daughter, known far and wide as Princess Kravess, married a real moron. But the Princess gets whatever she wants, and she wanted her husband to get a big job. So Kravess made him president of the cracker division. And now to prove how smart he is, Mr. Princess came up with the idea that because herring goes so well with crackers, he should own both companies. Kravess must know the guy's an idiot, but he's probably enjoying himself. When we were kids I was better than him at everything. I was picked first for the teams, he was picked last. I got the dolls, he got the dogs.

In spite of all that Harvard education, he's always wanted to stick it to me.

"Yesterday my herring was trading over the counter at eleven bucks a share. This morning Kravitco announced a hostile take over bid of fifteen dollars a share."

"Is that bad?" I asked.

"Listen, kiddo, herring is a gold mine. Forget about the fact that my kids and I pull out a nice living. I'm thinking of the future. I don't have to tell a smart boy like you about overpopulation, famine, and food shortages." Here, he stood up and started pacing the floor, waving his hands for emphasis as he spoke.

"The world needs protein. But look what's happening. Fish catches get smaller every year. Red meat has become the enemy. So where does the world turn?" He stood across from my desk and planted his hands to better stare at me.

There seemed only one obvious answer at the moment, so I gave it a try.

"Herring."

"You betcha. The world's greatest untapped resource."

Somehow I had difficulty visualizing little Somali children sitting in the mud while delicately nibbling the protein of the future in wine and cream sauce. But I encouraged him to go on.

"Listen. A tuna is a thing of beauty. A swordfish is glorious. But herrings are forever. Did you know that during the spawning season each female herring lays forty thousand eggs? If you don't catch a herring, it can live twenty years. You realize how many herring are out there? And for years they've been ignored; not too many people, I'm sad to admit, are regular herring eaters. I even remember my father singing that old Russian song: 'There are plenty of fish in the ocean, so why do you pick on me?

Feed borscht and salami to your Red Army, and let the herring to go free.'"

At the conclusion of this musical non sequitur, Finebloom sat down hard. For a moment, he looked dejected, then a fire reignited in his eyes.

"The great fortunes of this country were made by men who had a vision and an essential commodity. Rockefeller had oil. Carnegie had steel and Ford had cars. I have herring. And no business school bulvan is going to steal my birthright for a bowl of fifteen-dollars-a-share porridge."

Great fortunes, I thought. Carnegie, Rockefeller, and Ford. Why not give Sol a shot? What's so crazy about the idea of a Finebloom Foundation someday? I suppose I've heard stranger ideas. I applied the acid test. "What about thirty dollars a share?"

Finebloom sat back, solemnly stroked his chin, and then, in spite of previous tales of herring-do, looked up with a twinkling eye. "I wouldn't say no." He sat quietly for a moment. "I'm not getting any younger and my children aren't getting any smarter. What's the plan?"

For the next couple of weeks, I worked on nothing but Barry and Finebloom. Actually, I let Stromberg keep working on Barry and I turned my attention to Clupea Harengus Harengus (Atlantic herring).

Fine herring was in play, as they say on Wall Street, and when we counterattacked the price slowly worked its way up. We filed suit against Kravess; we alleged violation of SEC rules; we dragged out all the old claims about how his buyouts benefited only him while the stockholders got nothing; we had detectives following him and his family, and we searched for any type of knockout blow we could find. Battles for control of companies were not played out upon the gentlemanly fields of Eton. Rather, they're slugged out in the pits. We enjoined Kravess' tender offer and he won reversal on appeal. We made counteroffers and he sued us. After three weeks of daily litigation, the price of the shares had risen to twenty-three dollars each. Also, my client was happy to report, the sales of all types of herring, even the little bits, of which I am no particular fan, had doubled. Sales were up, the stock was up, but, alas, Kravess' bankroll was insurmountable. He kept buying and our majority kept shrinking.

Sol met with me daily (I had become his friend and confidant). We reviewed stockholder lists for allies. A number of mutual funds had pledged their allegiance to us. During one conference where we were reviewing stockholder lists, I pointed out to Sol that there seemed to be a number of single women in the Upper East Side who each owned one hundred shares. He shrugged his shoulders. "Man cannot live by herring alone." He assured me we would have their votes. We discussed every possible strategy and ended one night with my telling Sol to go out and find someone to make a friendly merger or buyout offer. We needed a white knight.

The next day he was late for our usual morning meeting and didn't show up until later that day. He came in with a man who could have passed as a Finebloom brother. He was little, neat, alert, and wore a metallic blue tie.

"Meet Weinlick," said Finebloom. "The answer to my prayers."

Mr. Weinlick stood smiling with a pleasant grin and nodded his head in agreement. He seemed a lovely old gentleman, but I couldn't imagine what prayer he was going to answer.

"He just flew in from Toronto," said Sol, as if that explained everything.

"That's true," said Mr. Weinlick, confirming my confusion.

"I can see you're not following. Listen," said Sol, and I did. "Last night I got home, tired and depressed. Pearl, my wife, who, if the truth must be known, hasn't been a source of much joy and cheer for about the last fifteen years, yells out from the kitchen. 'Sol, how's it going?' To which I replied as I sank in my favorite chair, 'Not good.'"

"That's true," nodded Mr. Weinlick, who had either heard this story before or was hiding in the kitchen with Pearl at the time.

Sol continued. "'What now?' yelled Pearl. I yelled back, 'After all we've been through now they tell me we need a white knight.'

"Now Pearl," he continued, "has lost more than just her looks, sense of humor and general joie de vivre over the years. Her hearing is going too. She yells back, 'I can't believe it; All day long herring, herring, herring, and now for supper you want white fish.'

"I was about to correct her, 'White knight, not white fish,' when I got a feeling like a lightning bolt right under my nose. Whitefish. That's the answer. Kravess wants to combine herring with crackers. I'll beat him to it. I'll merge with Whitefish. It's a natural horizontal integration. We can use the same sales force and we sell to the same distributors. The company would make no economic sense to Kravess and furthermore, whitefish isn't served with crackers. Maybe little rye slices, but not crackers."

"That's true," said Weinlick as animated as ever.

"Anyway," Sol continued as he paced the room, "there was only one man to call. My old friend Murray Weinlick of Weinlick's Whitefish and Smoked Delicacies— the biggest in North America. We talked all night. He flew in this morning and we made a deal."

I knew what was coming. "That's true," said Weinlick.

"Got any corporate lawyers around here who can type it up?" said Sol. I nodded. "We'll get the directors together, give it the stamp of approval, ram it through and we're home free."

"There may be some lawsuits," I said.

"You take care of that stuff," said Sol. "Meanwhile, I'm taking Weinlick out on the town. I got a couple a hundred shares of stock in my pocket. Who knows, maybe we'll get lucky." He delivered a playful elbow to Weinlick's side.

"Careful, Sol," I said as they walked to the door. "Your new partner may not be used to life in the fast lane."

"He'll learn," Sol said, putting his arm around Weinlick. "And besides," he said, turning back to me and winking as they walked out the door, "I'm not my brother's kipper."

YOUR DECORATOR SAYS

Trellised walls, with a sky and clouds painted on the ceiling, open up a bathroom and give it space.

TWENTY-FOUR

The Finebloom affair had consumed a good deal of my time. It was a nice rewarding diversion. I took care of the client and Stromberg was never far from Ally. I did well and she stayed well. But Barry's day of reckoning was getting closer. We had managed to get a few continuances of the trial date. There was no such thing as speedy justice in the Massachusetts courts. There were too many cases and too few judges working in a system as clogged as the arteries of a pastrami king. Every now and then court reform became a hot issue. But in a system where every job from file clerk to Chief Justice fell within some politician's appointment purview, reform would probably await revolution. In some cases, the entire defense strategy rests on delay, the idea being to put off a case for so long that it goes from some overworked assistant D.A.'s front burner, to back burner, to finally falling off the stove. At that point, the client ceases to be a criminal and becomes only a number on a file in a computer that has to be processed by a quick plea bargain. Unfortunately, murders seem to keep everyone's attention.

I had mostly convinced myself that Bristol was the killer, but mostly wasn't good enough. Frankie and Johnny were still possibilities, and I was sure I was missing something. Bristol would have been too simple a conclusion for the whole thing, and simple endings only occur in half hour TV shows; this was at least a miniseries. I wanted to start following people, hiring more private detectives, looking for DNA—the usual stuff in a criminal case. Ally, a student of Miss Jane Marple, who solved mysteries long before the discovery of DNA, thought we should invite everyone to dinner, which explains why I had left the office early on a Friday afternoon to help prepare for company, cocktails, conversation, and, who knows, maybe confession.

We had invited the unusual suspects: Barry, Billy Bristol, Steve and Bunny. Frankie and Johnny were also invited, but each begged off. Ally also thought we should throw in some diversions to make the whole thing less obvious, so she added a couple of single society decorator hangers on—Oatsie Thompson and Paige Watts. Oatsie and Paige were almost indistinguishable from each other. They were well bred, well married and well divorced. Both in their mid-forties, they were slim, fashionably elegant, and socially revered.

All in all, they were an interesting adjunct to the decorating world—not decorators, but definitely decorated. They, and others of their ilk, had townhouses in Boston, or brownstones in New York, as well as vacation homes in St. Barts, Palm Beach or Aspen. Because these homes were used for parties and fund-raisers for the socially prominent, their interiors could become famous. In a world where people still cared about place cards for dinner parties and men rotated dinner jackets so as not to be seen in the same suit two nights in a row, the Oatsies and Paiges of the world ruled. They were to the upper crust what rappers were to the 'hood—cultural icons to be worshipped and emulated. For decorators, they were even more important. Decorators found in them what renaissance artists sought from the Medicis—patronage, money, and legitimacy. But putting all that aside, when Ally confided in them that they could be part of an intimate supper with the alleged murderer Barry and a cast of questionable characters, they jumped at the chance to be part of a gossip's dream team.

Cocktails were called for seven, so naturally our guests arrived promptly at eight. Late arrival was such a given that the caterer had not even started setting up until seven. Barry was the first to arrive. As I had told him, we were dressing for dinner. He looked simply Fred Astaire-ish in a very conservative mode. Billy Bristol had a driver for the evening, so he fetched Oatsie and Paige and they all arrived together. Billy was dressed much like Barry. The girls could have been extras in the final cocktail scene of *Titanic* except that their jewelry was real and wouldn't have to be returned after the meal. Steve and Bunny offered the only color for the evening. She appeared to be very Versace, that is, very colorful and very skimpy. My view of fashion was that, with Bunny's body, she could skimp all she wanted. Steve looked like one of those producer types you see at the Academy Awards who make you wonder where people get purple shirts like that to go with lapel-less tuxedos. By eight thirty, we were all in the living room, drinking and chatting away.

The cocktail banter was restrained and polite. We covered such critical issues as architectural accessories (very in) and contemporary French furniture (always in). Our suspects seemed intent on avoiding the subject of Bruno or Megan. They walked through our house talking about the fabric on some antique chairs we had, deconstructed the drapery, and made idle interior design gossip.

"What do you think of our East Coast design world, Mr. Ashworth?" Oatsie asked Steve.

"It's really not that different from the West: Talented designers," he said, nodding to Ally; "Beautiful fabrics," nodding to a chair; "And a vision." I nodded to Bunny.

"And how do you like our Ally?" asked Paige. I did a quick nod at my wife lest she misconstrue my previous genuflection at the young Bunny.

"The best," he said. I loved Hollywood understatement. "I think that this time my vision will finally become a reality."

"You've had others?" Paige inquired.

"You bet," said Bunny—who may have been changing the subject until Ashworth brought it back on track.

"You know, Ms. Watts, L.A. isn't the cultural wasteland you think it is. I've worked with Megan, and before her Molly Parsons. I know you think we're barbarians, but we have show rooms and a Design Center. Sometimes we even get things ahead of Boston and New York."

This last remark seemed so unbelievable to Paige that, thankfully, she changed the subject to what I hoped would be the main topic for the evening,

"You know, Barry," she said between sips of her bourbon and branch water, "I've never had dinner with someone accused of murder. But frankly dear, I think you're innocent."

"That's very nice of you," Barry said, looking a little white around the gills.

"But then who do you think did it?" asked Oatsie as she held out her gin gimlet for a refill.

"Personally," said Paige, "I think it was done by a woman. I see passion written all over it. If you ask me, it was a woman who hated Megan."

The crash that came from the other side of the room diverted everyone's attention. Bunny was bending over a coffee table furiously wiping up the wine that had spilled from the now-broken glass she had dropped on the table. Bunny looked paler than Barry.

"Oh God, I'm so sorry," she said.

Ally jumped to her social rescue. "Don't worry, accidents happen."

"But the wine glass...."

"Forget it," said Ally. "We have eleven more just like it."

At which point the catering major domo announced that dinner was served and we all gratefully headed for the dining room.

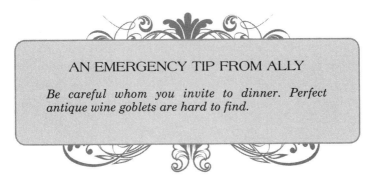

AN EMERGENCY TIP FROM ALLY

Be careful whom you invite to dinner. Perfect antique wine goblets are hard to find.

Ally had assigned us the traditional boy-girl arrangement, and we each took our places. Dinner was a simple affair. We were scheduled to start with marinated scallops and mussels on avocado, work our way through a rosette of New Zealand lamb and finish with a cold lime-zest soufflé. Based on the array of social skeletons before me, I was counting on leftovers.

"Getting back to the woman theory," said Bristol. "That would be a big help to you, wouldn't it, Barry?"

"I don't know how a woman would be strong enough to overpower Bruno," he responded.

"I'll bet she had a personal trainer," said Ashworth, giving us the breadth of his Los Angeles wisdom.

"Who had a trainer?" asked Bristol, somewhat confused.

"The lady killer," said Steve. "If she were in good shape, maybe an hour or two a day, she could have overpowered a sissy like Bruno. No offense, Barry."

"None taken."

"It's the dumbest theory I ever heard," said Oatsie.

"But if you're right, we have to look for an emotionally upset woman with a personal trainer."

"Talk about a redundant description," said Bristol, who added "no offense" when he noted the coming objection from the well-toned Paige.

"None taken," from Paige.

Ally and I furtively glanced at Bunny. We didn't know if she had killed anybody but we were afraid at what she would drop next. Luckily, all she dropped was her napkin, as she raced to the bathroom, stifling a sob.

Ally looked to Ashworth, "Can we do anything?"

"Nope. She just keeps getting upset over this Megan thing."

"Maybe she did it," said Oatsie to Billy.

"Maybe you did it," responded Billy.

Paige elbowed Billy in the ribs, "Oh, you rogue. Oatsie doesn't kill people, she just lets them know she took them off her invitation list. Then she watches them suffer."

This brought a round of laughter from the good-spirited table as Bunny returned making her apologies. "I'm so sorry everybody. I get so upset over Megan."

From where I was sitting, I couldn't help but see Paige lift her eyebrows to Oatsie, who nodded back. I looked over at Ally, who nodded at me to indicate that she had seen the same thing. When we all got up after dinner, I saw Ally head for Paige and engage her in a brief conversation. As our guests milled about, I pulled Ally aside.

"What gives?"

"Not much," she smiled. "Just an ugly rumor that Bunny's father had an affair with Megan, which ended badly right before his suicide."

I would have asked for more, but I noticed Justin standing on the top steps and waving down to us.

"Hey Dad," he yelled in a voice loud enough to draw everyone's attention. "It's Stromberg on the phone. He wanted me to give you a message."

"So, give."

"He says that Megan just woke up."

And here's what happened in the room: Barry let out a gasp and put his hand to his mouth, Billy crumpled up his napkin and threw it onto his plate, Bunny started crying again and ran for the bathroom, and Steve, who was still holding a dessert fork, looked at the departing Bunny and absentmindedly bent the fork in half. I hoped we had eleven more of those too. As for Oatsie and Paige, they looked thoroughly thrilled, as one said to the other, "Oh, what fun! Let's hurry home and make phone calls."

We ushered our guests out the door, and I ran to call Stromberg.

"What's the news?"

"Nothin'. I had a nurse on an informal payroll arrangement. She called me with the news. But I wouldn't rush over. Her eyes are open, but she can't speak. The doctors don't expect her to be able to communicate for several days. It's some sort of a post-coma state."

"Okay, this doesn't change much for the moment. Meet me in the office tomorrow. Let's do some investigating. There's a lot going on here and we've got to start narrowing things down."

TWENTY-FIVE

It was Monday and I was in my office at my usual perch, staring out the window. It looked like an early spring. The Red Sox hadn't returned from Florida yet, but the sun was warming the office. Looking down to the street, I could see that topcoats were off. A nice day to do some investigating, and Billy Bristol was a good place to start.

Stromberg and I had spent Sunday afternoon going over records of Bruno's payments to Claridge. We found Claridge's invoices for the Colombian fabrics and Bruno's checks to the phony BVI accounts. What was missing were records of the fabric delivery and the ultimate purchaser. We knew that Claridge's main office thought that Bristol was a genius with sales. We therefore assumed that he was actually making purchases of fabric. So much money was running through the accounts that actually buying some of the product would be a small cost. Obviously, he had someone in Latin America shipping him drugs in fabric. These "packages" must have gone to the shipping room that he was so anxious to keep me away from. Then they'd be parceled out among distributors. Finding these would be a nice link. Which was why, on this beautiful pre-spring day, I left my office to meet Stromberg on the corner. We were going on a stakeout.

I got into Stromberg's four-year-old blue Chevy when he stopped for the light. He took pride in buying American, using regular gas, and never needing repairs. The man had no style. What he did have was a digital camera, two thermoses, and a box of donuts.

"I suppose there's coffee in the thermoses," I said, buckling up.

"These are stakeout rations, boss. None of your fancy gourmet shit. We're real men on a real mission." I watched his expression as he said this, but whether he was serious was another mystery. We drove toward South Station and turned down Summer Street in the direction of the Design Building.

"So, boss, what are we looking for?"

"I'm not really sure. We'll go over and park behind the Claridge loading zone and see what happens. Maybe we'll see something that doesn't make sense."

"Makes sense," acknowledged my driver as he pulled into the Design Center.

"Go around the building and find a space where we can watch what happens," I said.

He did, and together we hunkered down for a day of watching and donuts. Boring is too gentle a word to describe the act of sitting in a parked car and staring at a loading dock. In a movie, this sort of thing only lasts a few minutes before something big happens. If they lasted four hours, the audience might grow restive. We were stuck watching cars and trucks pull up to the loading dock and writing down their descriptions in a notebook. From the looks of things, business was good at Claridge. Stromberg called out the vehicles and their license numbers as they pulled up and I took notes. That lasted for two hours and then we switched. On occasion, we took pictures.

By the end of the day, we had three pages of cars and trucks, a camera full of pictures, and no more donuts.

"Drive me back to my car," I said. "It looked like an ordinary bunch of delivery trucks, vans and station wagons, but I'll take the list and pictures home and see if there's any inspiration to be found."

Inspiration was all I would be finding at home that night. It appeared the kitchen had closed. Only the garbage bag, whose plastic sides lay in a deformed posture hugging the outlines of the ubiquitous pizza box, gave silent testimony to the dinner I missed.

"Your hero is home," I yelled upstairs.

"Justin," Ally yelled, "See who's here."

"Someone who says he's a wino," retorted the kid from the safety of upstairs.

"Hero," I said. "Hero!"

"Help, Mom, it's a homo."

"I give," I called. For effect, I added a well-worn Latin exhortation, "*O tempora, o mores.*"

"Hey mom," Justin yelled. "Now he says his name is Morris."

Showing no regard for the six jelly donuts that adhered to my innards, I dropped my briefcase and dashed (in a manner of speaking) up the stairs and into the den where I tackled Justin, who stood by the door, giggling. A charging, overweight, out of breath lawyer is more fearsome than feared, and Justin soon had me in a headlock.

"Fun's over, boys," said Ally as she walked out of the bedroom. "Justin, let your father go. If you hurt him, he'll complain all night."

I lay on the floor, assuming as dignified a position as possible while looking up at my beloveds. "Will you be serving me dinner here, or should I meet you downstairs?"

"I called your office and Lisa told me you'd be spending the day in a car with Stromberg eating donuts. I figured you'd be too full for a regular meal, so I thought perhaps a couple of your favorite olives would suffice."

"If they're surrounded by gin and vermouth they'll do quite nicely," I responded as we walked arm and arm downstairs, leaving Justin to his alleged studying.

I stretched out on a living room couch where Ally met me with my dinner. Sitting there, martini in hand, I imagined myself a character in a black and white movie. Dick Powell, Fred Astaire and me. Elegantly holding our drinks, we bantered and badinaged, playing out our idyllic lives. Were martinis better in the movies? Was life better in black and white? My reveries were interrupted by living color. "So, tell me about your day," said neither Myrna Loy nor Cyd Charisse.

"We came, we sat, we watched. Nothing too exciting about this detective business. Made a few lists, took a few pictures."

"A regular snooper. Let me see a few close-ups."

"If delivery people excite you, be my guest." I took a group of pictures from the inside pocket of my jacket and spread them out on the hand-painted coffee table that had never, at least in this decade, seen coffee or any other liquid with staining qualities.

I picked one up and held it out.

"Here's a great shot of a red truck," I offered.

"Interesting," said Ally as she looked at the picture.

"You've never seen a delivery truck?" I asked.

"Not the truck, Shamus. Over in the side of the picture, the blond by the blue Volvo. That's Patsie Winthrop. I wonder what she was doing there."

"Picking up some fabric," I suggested.

"Patsie's pickups are usually more animated than fabric. She's a big deal in the League. *Très* snooty—I would have thought errands were beneath her. Let me see some more pictures."

Ally leafed through another group of shots before stopping at one. "Here. Look," she said, holding out the picture.

"It's your friend Patsie again."

"To begin, she's no friend. But if you look you'll see that her car is parked in a different space and this time she's getting out. Perhaps she came and went." Ally was getting into it and now studied the shots with more interest.

"Here's another one," she exclaimed, punching my arm with excitement.

I looked at the picture. In this shot another woman was standing by another Volvo station wagon while a man was placing a bolt of fabric in the back. "I suppose you know who this is?" I asked.

"No doubt about it, Hercule. This little pug-nosed wonder is Willie Potts. The League's treasurer."

She jumped up and ran to a small Queen-somebody writing desk in the corner of the room. Returning with a silver antique magnifying glass, which to my knowledge had never magnified anything except its own price, she examined the last picture. In a transition from decorating homes to Sherlock Holmes, she uttered the well-worn, "Aha."

"'Aha' what?"

"Look what I've found."

And I did. Sure enough, the fabric that Willie was loading into her Volvo, and the corner of fabric that could be seen in Patsie's Volvo, were both from the increasingly popular Claridge Latin American collection.

TWENTY-SIX

Several things struck me as rather hard to believe. It was inconceivable that Patsie and Willie, or anyone in their understated circle, would actually decorate with Latin American floral prints. A pillow for the maid's room maybe, but nothing more. It was also impossible to imagine that these pillars of the Women's League were mixed up with Columbian drugs, not to mention a dose of murder and mayhem. Their ancestors may have made their fortunes in rum and slaves, but the last couple of hundred years had cleansed the bloodlines.

There was, however, no good explanation. During the next week, Stromberg resumed his high caloric stakeout. Both Patsie and Willie showed up two more times. On each occasion, they drove off in station wagons with similar bolts of cloth. Stromberg kept at it and started to follow them when they left the Design Center, and his reports at that point were curiouser still. They each drove north, over the Mystic River Bridge and into Saugus. This was certainly an unusual route for these two. Saugus was a very working-class suburb, resplendent with half-empty strip malls and discount warehouses. It was quite an unusual venue for Boston Leaguers.

They stayed on Route 1 until they reached a group of low buildings behind a sign that said, "Saugus Self Storage." Their routine was always the same. The self-storage facility was comprised of a series of long, low metal buildings with garage-like doors. Each time they arrived they went to a different door and with a key, opened the door and deposited the packages. They then left the premises and could be seen putting the keys into envelopes which they then deposited in a nearby mailbox before traveling home.

When Stromberg made his report, we were both excited about the possibilities.

"No doubt about it, boss," Stromberg said. "These society broads are distributing coke."

"In the realm of the hootsie tootsie, they're all toot," I added. "What we've got to do is close the circle. We've got to stake out the storage center to see who makes the final receipt. Take pictures. I'm thinking of joining you and seeing if we can get the goods."

"This could be expensive."

"Don't worry, Barry's not against spending money to avoid a life sentence."

Stromberg smiled. "Just so you know, this is Saugus—Hilltop Steakhouse, Weylu's, the Ship. No donuts, boss. When I stake out in Saugus, I stake out in class."

I squeezed his smiling cheek. "Eat all you want, *bubeleh*. Just take some nice pictures and don't smear any butter on the lens."

Stromberg did better than I expected. It was also much stranger than I expected.

Four days later, I was in my office when Lisa announced the arrival of Stromberg. Saugus appeared to have treated him well.

"Peter," I said, "I think you're having a growth spurt, which, if you were fifteen, would be fine. But at the age of forty-eight, it may not be that blessed an event. Did anyone ever tell you that man cannot live by fried clams, tenderloin tips, and moo goo gai pan alone?"

"You left out pizza."

"Was there pizza, too?" I asked.

"More than you'll ever know. Look at these."

Stromberg spread out a series of prints on my desk. They were pictures of pizza trucks; more specifically, Dante's Divine Pizzas, a relative newcomer in the Domino's/Little Caesars quick pizza market. There were also pictures of Dante's Divine delivery people. What was unusual was that instead of delivering the ever-popular double cheese with pepperoni to your friends and neighbors, these fellows were all pictured using keys to open Saugus Self Storage bins and carrying rather garish bolts of fabric to the back of Dante's Divine delivery trucks, after which they each made a hasty exit.

"Is it time to bring in the police?" Peter asked.

"I'm not sure. What have we got? So far we all we have is the most unusual pizza and fabric delivery system in America. We haven't seen a drug. In addition, the Boston Women's League has a generous helping of husbands with substantial clout. No policeman with any hope for a career is going to get involved. My instinct says that we can get great mileage from all this at the trial, although fitting the pieces together is still a bit tricky. I also think we need actual proof that when Dante delivers a pizza and a Coke, there's no liquid involved.

"We still have a couple of weeks to go," I added. "Plenty of time for everything to fall into place. What bothers me about this is that we've never explained the presence of Dr. Zaid. Remember the guy we met at Show House? That event is long over, but the good or bad Doctor is apparently ensconced in Beacon Hill, doing what?"

"I could break into his house. Search the place."

"No, thanks. I don't need another case when you get caught. We may have to bend a few laws in Saugus, but the

Beacon Hill security is bound to be much better. Why don't we just walk up and ring the doorbell? If he's home, we'll improvise. Bottom line is maybe if the guy is mixed up in this whole thing, our presence will cause ripples that could become some kind of wave for our side. Who knows, maybe we'll find him entertaining Bunny and then the plot will really thicken."

"Where do you think she fits into all of this?"

"Who knows? But every time Megan's name is mentioned she either breaks a household item or decapitates a plant. I haven't taken her off my list."

"And Ashworth?"

"Just another Hollywood schmuck."

"Maybe, boss. We'll see. Let's get started."

I looked over at Stromberg who looked willing to go. The grueling task of sitting still and eating for hours on end had been unkind to my snooper. It was a good thing his pants were polyester; natural fibers had limited stretch. He would never make it up the hill on foot. We left my office, grabbed a cab, and in a few moments were back at the scene of the crime. I decided that the direct approach was the only approach, so Peter and I climbed the steps. Finding no doorbell, we used the brass sheep's head hanging on the front door for its intended purpose and knocked.

The door was opened. The opener, as large as the door itself, filled most of the available space. To my untraveled eye, he looked Middle Eastern. If that were so, he was likely a major force in Saudi Arabian football. For all I knew, he was bigger than Bahrain.

"May I help you?" he asked with politeness that I was sure was more tutored than sincere.

"We'd like to see Dr. Zaid, if he's at home," I said as I heard a voice call out from behind this door keeper.

"Who is it, Alfred?"

"Alfred?" I couldn't help myself from echoing.

The not-so-gentle giant actually looked embarrassed. "The doctor makes a joke all the time. Since coming to this country he has become a fan of your Batman." Then he stiffened, "What do you want?"

What's a lawyer without a business card? I handed him one of mine. Without turning from his post, he glanced down at the card and then back at us. "It is a lawyer named Levin," he called to the voice inside.

I heard a movement and the behemoth turned away from his post to reveal his boss, smiling and welcoming us into the house. We entered and the door closed. I introduced Stromberg and we were ushered into the living room.

The house was exactly as I had last seen it. Usually the decorators removed their furniture and furnishings after the house tour was over and the owner's only benefits were new paint and wallpaper. I remembered Ally telling me that the buyer of this house wanted everything. Each decorator was called by a banker, who asked for the prices and sent a check. No muss, fuss, or dickering. We sat down and I held back the urge to pat the very familiar stone dogs that stared at me.

Dr. Zaid must have noticed my glance. "Ah yes, Mr. Levin. This room must appear familiar to you. I believe I bought it from your wife. But tell me, what brings you to my home?"

"You know, Doctor," I began, "about the crimes that took place here. I'm representing the accused. The trial is starting soon. I haven't been here in so long, I thought if I could walk through some of the rooms again, look in the basement, things like that, I might see some things that escaped the police."

Dr. Zaid leaned back in his chair. He was dressed casually in slacks, sweater, and shoes, no socks. I had the feeling that he purchased his clothes like his furniture—whatever he saw on the mannequin, he bought. Today's outfit indicated that he walked by a Polo window recently.

Dressed in American prep clothes, Dr. Zaid cut a far different figure than in the shapeless robes I had seen him in previously. He was trim and fit. A pencil thin mustache on a face that was a bit too tanned and weathered to indicate any fear of ozone depletion. Similarly, like so many third-worlders who grew up in countries without surgeon generals, he was smoking. He took a drag and, as he exhaled, told me, "I'm afraid that would be quite impossible."

No reason was given, but since the hulk from the door had positioned himself behind me I felt that cross-examination was inappropriate.

"Well," I said, rising from the chair. "Thank you for your time. We had better get back and prepare for trial."

Dr. Zaid also rose. "I enjoy watching your Court TV in this country. It is interesting to see how you lawyers get guilty people off. How will you do that in this case?"

I looked him squarely in the eye. "Why, that's easy. I'll have to convince the jury that someone else did it. By the way, how did your business deal with Billy Bristol work out?"

Odd Job's Mediterranean cousin took a step toward me. The Doctor gave an almost imperceptible shake of his head. "You are to leave now, Mr. Levin. No more questions. I have never understood the informality of your country, but I advise you to mind your own business. Good day."

"Don't upset yourself, Doctor," I said as we walked out of the room. "I didn't come for a fight, just a harmless little kibitz."

At this, Alfred became even more agitated. He stepped forward and grabbed me by the collar. "You've got no proof. It wasn't me," he stammered. "I would never harm a kibbutz."

Stromberg took a step toward us and Zaid let loose a stream of Arabic. Alfred let go and retreated.

"You will have to excuse my man," Zaid said, taking my arm and moving me faster to the door. "He is not sufficiently worldly to appreciate the difference between a trite Yiddish word and an illegal outpost of Zionism on occupied territory. Alfred burns for his Palestinian cousins, but the burning is only symbolic." When we reached the front door, he added, "I advise you not to upset Alfred or, for that matter, me." The door slammed.

"So much for fabled Arabian hospitality," I said to Peter as we started walking down Beacon Hill. "I'm no detective, but he seemed merely unfriendly until we mentioned the murder and Bristol, and then things got hostile."

"What was with the Bristol business deal?"

"I don't know. It was an inspiration that worked. I thought we could try to rattle him a bit, and he certainly lost his Ralph Lauren desert cool. While we're inspired, let's drive out to Saugus. I'd like to see the operation for myself."

We walked down the hill to my garage. Stromberg was huffing and puffing all the way, proving that when you're really out of shape, breathing hard is not just an uphill reaction. If we won this case and got a large enough bonus, I would send Stromberg to a spa. If we lost, I just wouldn't pay him. Either way, he'd have to eat less.

TWENTY-SEVEN

We got into my car and drove out over the Mystic River Bridge, up Route 1 toward the self-storage. Peter gazed ruefully at the plastic cows, neon burgers, and giant Pagodas we passed. These were all tantalizing symbols of the gargantuan platters of food that could be had within. He showed no emotion, however, when we drove by The Golden Banana, the area's hottest strip club. I was beginning to worry about him.

Our destination was on the other side of the Banana, and as we cut through its parking lot, my trip immediately began to pay off. There, sneaking out the back door, with a hat pulled down not far enough to hide his face, was the Honorable Elijah Adams himself. I hadn't seen him since he set Barry's bail. I certainly never expected to see him here. This sighting was all the more remarkable because I distinctly remembered the sign over the front door advertising today as Chippendale Day, the all-male nude review. Scratch a homophobe and you never know what you'll find. I tucked this information away for future use, although the Judge would probably claim he was doing research.

Stromberg directed me through the Banana parking lot to a side street. From there, we turned onto a driveway which caused us to double back until we were parked behind a couple of trash bins parallel to the front of Saugus Self Storage.

"This is where I've been doing my watching," Peter said. "Get out of the car and we can kneel behind those barrels over there."

I followed his directions and put myself in a position that left me well hidden but with a clear view. I wasn't prepared for a long wait. We had no food and I had forgotten to bring a book or newspaper. Luckily, Stromberg nudged me after a couple of minutes.

"Here she comes."

A blue Volvo station wagon passed in front of us. The license plate was three digits. Low number plates like this in Massachusetts were passed down through family lines. This number, 318, indicated that one of the driver's ancestors received the three hundred and eighteenth plate ever issued. *It was ironic*, I thought, *that the car's driver might, someday, end up making license plates.* Of course, she would be turning out six-digit plates. It would be a different life indeed, common labor for the common man. The bumper stickers went well with the plate: "Go Wellesley Soccer" was pasted over "Pro-Choice is Pro-Life." Just the right blend of responsible suburban elitism. There was a Harvard Club parking sticker on the rear window.

The car pulled over to one of the storage units' pull-down doors. The car door opened and the long, tanned legs that languorously swiveled out and down heralded the disembarkation of Willie Potts. She got out, walked to the rear of the car and opened the station wagon's rear gate. Taking out a couple of bolts of fabric, she opened the storage door, stowed away the fabric, locked the door and got back into her car. She then drove to the exit where there was a row of mailboxes. She pulled up beside one, lowered her window, deposited the key, closed the mailbox and drove away.

"Not that I ever doubted you, Peter, but this is truly amazing."

"The whole thing beats the crap outta me, boss. What's this world coming to when a classy society broad acts the same as some regular lowlife?"

"I don't know. Maybe it's democracy run amok. We'll philosophize tomorrow. Tonight's for detective work. It's starting to get dark, so this is as good a time as any. Let's get the key."

Peter and I got back into my car and drove over to the mailbox. It was unlocked and contained only the aforementioned key, which I took.

"What's the plan, boss?"

"I can think of only one. We'll put the car back out of sight, run over to the storage locker and take a look. How often do the pizza guys come for pickups?"

"There's no real schedule," said Stromberg. "We better be careful."

I drove back to the garbage bins and parked. It was dark. Stromberg took a thin flashlight out of his pocket and we made our way quickly over to the door. The key fit in the lock and in a matter of seconds the door was up and we were looking at rows of rolled fabric bolts.

"Now what?" Peter asked.

"Unless I misguessed, you're the kind of guy who not only carries a flashlight at all times, but would never leave home without a Swiss army knife. So if you could do the honors, we can open up one of these rolls and see the surprise inside."

I was not wrong. Peter took out a Swiss Army knife, and, after passing up the toenail cutter, tooth pick, magnifying glass, and can opener, found just the right blade to slit open the bottom of one of the rolls. We both kneeled down, our backs to the road, to look for the treasure. Peter made a small puncture wound in the bottom of one of the rolls and a thin stream of white powder spilled out. I quickly stuck my finger in the hole.

"Peter, push some of that packing tape back over this hole. I don't want anyone to know this has been opened," I said as I withdrew my finger.

"You think it's the real stuff?" he asked.

"Only one way to find out." I shrugged my shoulders and rubbed the finger covered with white dust over the front of my gums. I looked over at Stromberg.

"It's the real stuff."

Just then a flash of headlights crossed above us.

"As they say in the movies, Peter, we've got company."

Peter looked back over his shoulder. "It's a Pizza truck! They'll start opening all the mailboxes until they find the key. Now what?"

"You stay here," I whispered. "Time for more inspiration."

Before he could protest, I pushed him into the storage room and pulled down the door. Then I took off running toward the mailboxes and the truck.

"Hey, you guys!" I yelled. "Where the hell you been? We've been waiting thirty minutes."

The window on the passenger side came down. A pock-marked face with slicked-back black hair emerged.

"What the fuck you want, man?"

"Two large cheese, one with anchovies and one without," I said.

"What the fuck you talkin' about?"

I could see that this was not going to be a battle of wits. If there were to be any battle at all it would probably involve weapons, and I had left Stromberg's Swiss Army knife with him. As for me, I had only my wits, and they would have to do.

"We called thirty minutes ago and ordered two large pizzas. Delivery was guaranteed within twenty minutes."

At this the face pulled back into the cab of the truck. I could overhear a muffled conversation. The head reemerged.

"Who the fuck is 'we'?"

"Some guys from my Tae Kwan Do class. School's out for the season, so we're putting our nun-chucks, throwing stars, and ceremonial swords in storage. So, how about those pizzas?"

The head pulled back and more conversation ensued before it stuck back out again.

"How the fuck long you fucking guys gonna be here?"

"We're just waiting for our food and then we're on our way."

"We ain't got no fuckin' anchovies."

"Gee," I said, "the guys are awfully hungry. What have you got?"

The door opened and the face, along with adjoining body, emerged. He was about my height, black turtleneck and black jeans. He walked around to the back of the truck and I followed. He opened a panel and looked in.

"We got fucking pepper-fuckin'-roni."

"I guess it'll have to do, but I'm not paying."

"Over my fuckin' dead body."

"Listen my good man, I watch TV—I see your ads. If the delivery isn't made in twenty minutes, the pizza is free."

A menacing step toward me was halted by a yell from inside the truck.

"Louie, what the fuck is going on?"

From his speech pattern, I deduced they were from the same tribe. The aforementioned Louie walked back around to the driver's side, and from his flailing of arms, I could see that a dispute of some kind had developed. Louie walked back to the opened panel, reached in and pulled out two pizza cartons.

"Here's your fucking pepperoni." After which he gave me a cold but contrived stare, climbed back into the truck, and they drove away.

When they were out of sight, I raced back to the storage bin and pushed open the door. Stromberg was sitting on the floor smiling.

"Let's go." I said. "They'll be back."

He jumped up and we closed the door. We ran to the car, put the pizzas in the back and drove the key up to the mailbox. In another minute, we were headed south on Route 1, toward home.

"So," I said. "Not a bad night's work, if I do say so."

Stromberg sat silently.

"And free pizza. Peter, reach back and get us a slice or two."

"No time for food," was his response. I looked over at him. Could this be? Peter was passing on food? And then another memory of thirty years ago came back.

"Say Peter...while you were waiting in that storage room I assume you cleaned up all the evidence that spilled."

"Cleaned it? When you pushed me back and closed the door I fell face first into it." He wiped his nose and mouth with the same arm motion.

"So," I said, "it's clean as a whistle?"

And as I looked at him he began to whistle. It wasn't easy to whistle *The Best of Bob Dylan*, but it carried us all the way back to Boston.

TWENTY-EIGHT

I returned home around nine o'clock that night. Ally's car was missing from the driveway. Justin met me at the door.

"At last," he said as I walked in.

"You missed me. I'm honored."

"I have to do a book report on King Lear and I need proofreading."

"I once had a case like King Lear," I said as Justin grabbed my elbow and pushed me in the direction of his room. "A wealthy father divided up stock in the family corporation between his three kids. Then two of the three voted to fire him and throw him out of the company apartment in Manhattan. Even took away his company car. Now that was a tragedy."

"Very funny, Dad. Makes me want to howl with laughter. Howl, howl, howl."

"That's impressive. You've actually read the play. I'm looking forward to a little proofreading."

I sat in Justin's room, scrolling down his computer screen, adding a comma here and a semicolon there. I had just finished and Justin had gone off to sleep when I heard the door open downstairs.

"Hey, Buzzy baby, come downstairs for news."

Ah, my beloved. Taking leave of my lad, I ambled down to my lady. She was just closing the refrigerator door and stood, grapes in hand, as I entered the room.

"What's up?" she asked. "I called Justin an hour ago to say goodnight and make sure Maria was on the job. He told me you hadn't gotten home yet."

"I must have just missed you. I've had a full day investigating and proofreading King Lear."

"So, do you know who did it?"

"I think it was Goneril and Regan."

"Very funny. Now for some real news—you'll never guess where I've been," she said, popping a grape in her mouth.

"Not the heath," I responded. "I've just been upon it with Justin and you were nowhere to been seen."

"Cut the Ivy League bullshit. I just got back from visiting hours at the MGH."

"No. Megan?"

"You bet. While you were out playing detective, Oatsie called to tell me that she had just heard from the wife of a surgeon that Megan had started talking. So, team player that I am, I thought I could cheer up dear Megan, and find a few clues for the team."

"And...."

"And, it gets even better. I go up to Megan's room, and I guess the news hadn't broken yet, because there was no one else there. So, I sit down next to the bed, just me and Megan for a chat. But it wasn't much of a conversation because she's still pretty gaga."

I grabbed a few grapes and encouraged Allyn to continue.

"I sat down and said hello to her. She looked at me somewhat vaguely, and asked me how I liked the room. She sat up a little and pointed around the room. I told her it was lovely and she started telling me how it was going to be photographed for a magazine. She's so out of it she thinks she's at the Show House, not a hospital."

"Alas, poor Megan."

"I thought you were doing Lear, not Hamlet."

"When I'm in an Elizabethan mood, there's no stopping me. Tell me more."

"I will," she said, finishing the last grape and boosting herself up to sit on the counter. This boost caused her skirt to ride nicely up her legs. If I wasn't excited before, I was now. I walked closer, moving in for the thrill.

"Anyway," she continued, "I'm sitting there wondering what to say next, when all of a sudden the door opens and in walks Bunny."

"It gets better and better," I said. This was true because I had now positioned myself between Ally's legs which were dangling over the counter. My right hand was under her delightful derriere and with my left I was stroking her face.

"Bunny comes into the room, and acts like I'm not even there. She walks over to the bed, leans over Megan and starts screaming at her. Things like, 'You should be dead' and 'I'll kill you, bitch.'"

"Unbelievable," I said, now repositioning my right hand and moving my left down from the hair for more important work. "What happened next?"

"So at this point Megan sits bolt upright, stares at Bunny, lets out a high-pitched scream, and passes out. A nurse and an orderly run into the room, see what's going on and they grab Bunny, who faints dead away."

"Tell me more." I said. At this point I need not say that Ally's hands were as actively involved with me as mine were with her.

"More," she said a bit flushed, "More. Oh, what more is there? They checked Bunny in for observation, Megan was out cold again, and I came home."

"You know," I said, nuzzling her ear. "Bunny's role in all this is becoming a major dilemma."

"Some detective," she said nuzzling right back. "You know, I think you finally put your finger on it."

And sure enough, I had. Talk about howl.

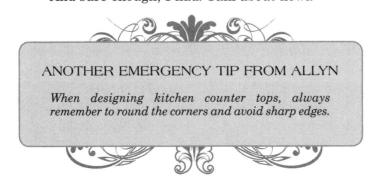

ANOTHER EMERGENCY TIP FROM ALLYN

When designing kitchen counter tops, always remember to round the corners and avoid sharp edges.

Later that night, Ally was watching the news and I sat in the den, thinking about the case. The essential ingredient in preparing for trial is the development of what my law school professors referred to as the "theory of the case." Good strategy encompasses more than just presenting evidence and making hostile witnesses look bad on cross examination. You need a purpose and you need a method. Everything a good lawyer does, from the bailiff's opening "Hear ye, hear ye" to the verdict, should be calculated to achieve a result. If a trial were a play, even the ad-libs would be prepared in advance.

Because the jury is watching you throughout the proceedings, there's no detail that cannot be used for some purpose. For example, when the judge calls you and opposing counsel up for a sidebar conference away from the jury to settle an argument or make a ruling, always appear to be the winner. No matter how badly his Honor slams you, walk away with a firm but determined smile. On the rare occasion when your entire case has been cut out from under you, it is especially important, when breaking from the huddle, to subtly touch your opponent on the shoulder as if to show a victor's good sportsmanship. Not only do you appear to be the winner, but the jury perceives the other side as the loser. By itself, this sidebar game won't turn a loss to a win, but it's one firm brushstroke in the picture you're trying to paint.

And it is the big picture that should be the focus of preparation. When Barry's trial starts, what was it that I wanted the jury to see? What was my theory? Sometimes a defense was nothing more than making the prosecution prove its case beyond a reasonable doubt. We may have no exculpatory evidence ourselves, so all we can do is cast doubt on the eyewitness, show the forensic evidence to be open to various interpretations, and never let our client utter a word. White-collar crimes involving stocks and bonds can sometimes simply be defended with an array of accountants and investment bankers who are just as credible as the prosecution's experts.

As I thought more about this, I realized, not for the first time, that the only advantage a trial lawyer has over a football coach is that he can plea bargain. Imagine one team telling the other that in exchange for not fighting it out for a full game, possibly injuring some good players, and maybe even winning, a deal could be struck. In exchange for the anticipated loss of twenty-one to nothing, the losing team would agree to stop playing if they could, say, only lose three to nothing. Bookies could probably form a strong lobby against sports bargaining.

In Barry's case, plea bargaining was never an issue because Barry refused to consider it. The prosecution's case was circumstantial and they probably would have come up with a deal that offered Barry about seven years in jail. He would have none of it. Therefore, I was in my study at home ready to develop a winning theory.

Our investigation had turned up dirt under every antique area rug. The Women's League appeared to be the high society version of an evil empire. Billy Bristol was using a legitimate decorative fabric business to import drugs and launder money. Bruno and Megan were dirty

players. The mysterious Dr. Zaid was somehow involved
with Bristol, but was he involved with everything else that
appeared crooked? Bunny could have been a crazed killer
and I wasn't too thrilled with Ashworth. I found out that
Frankie and Johnny really were lovers; but could they also
be the killers? These were all facts and great questions, but
none of them would give us the real killer. In truth, Barry
still could have done it. The unlawful pursuits of the
victims were neither a defense nor grounds for a
substantial discount when it came to sentencing. I could
certainly confuse the jury, and perhaps even create
something approximating reasonable doubt, but, as we
used to say in the '80s, more would be better.

I was sitting on the floor, surrounded by notes and
pictures of evidence, victims and crime scenes. Lost in
thought though I was, I noticed Ally come into the room.
Just what I needed. Apparently, earlier events had only
been an appetizer. She was wearing a classic Gothic
romance outfit. Black silk lounging garments hung
provocatively on her still supple frame; no hint of
undergarments; a simple strand of pearls. She looked at
me. I looked at her. With her tongue, she moistened her lips
in a clockwise circle. I returned the moistening,
counterclockwise. She winked at me with her left eye. I
winked back with my right. She lifted her right eyebrow. I
lifted both eyebrows—an utter failure. I tried for one
eyebrow again but both kept popping up. She had me, I was
a loser in pre-foreplay facial seduction. I tried for the left
eyebrow, but could still only raise both at once. She was
Aphrodite. I was Groucho Marx. "Care to join me on the
rug?" I offered.

"Can we search for clues together?"

"In every nanny and crook."

"Isn't that cranny and nook?" she said as she
deliciously brought her face down to mine and slowly
pushed me back. Two horizontal planes.

"Top man," she said, kissing me.

"Bottom man," I responded. Some Three Stooges lines live forever. I kissed her and she lifted her head to brush back her hair. She lay on top of me. We were like two Lincoln logs, one on top of the other awaiting the connector log to lock them firmly in place. I looked up at her. She looked down at me.

She looked up. "Wait a minute, what's this?" she said.

"After all these years, not to mention your background in high school biology, you still have to ask?"

"Not that," she said. "This." She was pointing to some color pictures behind my head.

"Pictures, evidence, whatever," I responded. "Forget them. We've got our own Kodak moment going here."

"Put your paws on pause," Ally said. "I want to see these."

I felt the moment pass and sat up as Ally crawled off me. As they say, "The best planned lays of mice and men...."

We were both lying on our stomachs, propped up on elbows as we looked over the pictures. "These beauties I know you remember, our friends, the victims."

"A memory I can do without," Ally said. "Anything less gruesome?"

I fanned out a group of prints. "Here we have the weapons. Several views of tassel cords formerly adorning the neck of Bruno. Nothing special about them, generally available to the decorative world."

I picked up the next group. "And here we have the instrumentalities of La Smash de Megan. Hammer, I believe a Craftsman. There must be two million just like it. And lastly, a few shots of the cloth that wrapped the head that got hammered. I'm sure there's a million yards of this stuff around too."

"Let me see those cloth pictures," Ally said, taking them from me and looking closer. She rolled over on her back holding the pictures straight out.

"Do you know what I'm thinking?" she asked.

"I haven't a clue," I responded.

"Wrong. As a matter of fact, you've got one hell of a clue right here."

"Where?"

"Look at that cloth, *chéri*. What do you see?"

"Some blood stains and flowers and fruit."

"Absolutely," she said, now getting up on her knees. "But not just any flowers and fruit. This design is part of the Claridge Fleurs et Fruit series."

"So?"

"So, Sherlock, you remember that Megan was almost murdered in September 2006."

"Certainly." I was beginning to feel uncomfortable as I sensed that top man was about to earn her position.

"Well, my own little inspector Clouseau," she continued, obviously relishing the revelation that was to come. "The Fleurs et Fruit line just happens to be Claridge's biggest seller in 2007."

"So, there's tons of it around."

"Perhaps," she said licking her lips, this time from deduction not seduction, "but the line wasn't put in the Boston showroom until November 1, 2006. So two months earlier, the general public wouldn't have had access to that particular cloth. It seems that your murderer made a rather poorly planned design decision."

I was astounded. "You know what this means?" I said.

"It means," she said as she slowly reclined, grabbing my shirt, "that you can take yourself off pause. And Buzz," she added, looking up at me as she had somehow moved to the bottom, "as long as you're sitting there with your mouth open, be a dear and think of something to do with it. And Buzz, while you're thinking, remember what they taught you in real estate law: location, location, location."

Ah Allyn, a clue *and* you. What a night. It's a good thing that all the walking in this case was keeping me in shape.

WHEN REPAINTING, REMEMBER

A blush of pink for walls in any room is flattering for skin colors.

TWENTY-NINE

The next morning, I had to meet a client for breakfast to pick up some papers. Barry's trial was scheduled to start in two days. In a week, it would be history, and the business of the law had to keep moving. Nevertheless, I left the house early so that I could make a quick stop to see if Bunny was alright and talkative. Ally was off to Nantucket for the day with Ashworth, so I could only give her emotional support. I drove to the hospital, got a good early space in the garage, and found my way to Bunny's room.

She had a private room on the same pretentious floor as Megan. I walked in and found her sitting up in bed, drinking tea. She was wearing a hospital robe, no makeup and her hair was hanging uncombed over her face. In short, she looked phenomenal (in shorts, even better). She looked over at me when I entered.

"Oh Buzz, you didn't have to come. I'm getting out of here this morning. They just wanted to keep me for observation after last night."

"How are you?"

"I'm fine, but I feel like such a total idiot."

"You don't have to answer me, but what's with you and Megan? Strange things happen to you when she's around—even when her name's mentioned."

"It's totally awful," she said, tears streaming down her face. "I can't even talk about it, but I'm just going to say it fast and get it over with. Last year when she was in L.A., she was decorating for my parents as well as Steve. My father fell for her, they had a major affair, and he left my mother. I guess he thought that he and Megan were going to move in together or something, but she dumped him. He tried to get back with my mother, but she was too hurt and too bitter. He couldn't face being such a fool and so alone. He was depressed and one night he just—"

"You had good reason to hate her," I said. "So, why were you visiting her in the hospital? I remember you were reading to her."

"Oh," she said, sitting up and running her hand through her hair to brush it out of her face. "I didn't want to come. That was all Steve. He said we should channel our negative energy away from Megan, that we would recover if she recovered. Totally bogus, if you ask me."

"What did he need to recover from?"

"Oh, like, he really hated Megan. Steve told me that my father and I and he were all victims of Megan. Yeah, right. My father's dead, I want to kill her, and Steve's mad because she screwed up his decorating."

"That's why he feels like a victim?"

"He's, like, more than a little weird on the subject of Megan and decorating. He fired her because she couldn't capture his vision. I honestly don't know how your wife puts up with him. The decorator he fired before Megan gave up the business. No one's even seen the guy for a year."

"So, why do you put up with him?"

"He was good to me when I was really low. So I figure I owe him something. He's a big-time producer—we travel and it's fun until he buys a house and starts decorating. Then it's this 'vision' bullshit. Maybe I've had it."

"You know, Bunny, I'm representing the guy charged with attempting to murder the person you wanted to kill. Where were you the night Megan was attacked?"

Here she looked up at me with those big blue eyes and, smiling, said, "I just can't remember. Should I?"

"It wouldn't hurt," I said, walking to the door. "Oh, by the way, when you and Steve were here to see Megan and we all left together, did either of you come back into the hospital?"

"Oh yeah, how funny. We both got into the limo and then one of us had to go back in to use the bathroom. So the other went too."

"Who had to go first, you or Steve?"

She looked straight at me. "Gee, I can't remember that either. Should I?"

"It wouldn't hurt," I said, leaving the room. "It wouldn't hurt."

I was in my car and off to my breakfast appointment with even more questions than answers. I drove up Cambridge Street, over Beacon Hill to Beacon Street, and around the Public Gardens. Newbury Street in the early morning was always a delight. Usually, Boston's most fashionable shopping street was mobbed. But at nine thirty, none of the stores were open yet and there were plenty of parking spaces. I turned up from Arlington Street and parked at the side of the Ritz. Four quarters in the meter bought me an hour of street time and I went into the cafe. Next month's problem was sitting at a window table for two, already eating breakfast. She was well dressed, well coifed, and well off. Middle age had been kind to her and life truly began at forty-five—that was when her seventy-two-year-old husband finally did the right thing and, in a room of this very Ritz, dropped dead in the arms of a very expensive and very surprised exotic dancer. This, in turn, left my client, Madeleine, very relieved and very rich: Relieved, because she didn't actually have to meet the mercenary whose ad she had answered in *Soldier of Fortune* and to whom she was prepared to pay $100,000 to kill her husband, and rich because that's what widows of the fabulously wealthy become on the occasion of these blessed events.

No tears were shed at the passing of Madeleine's beloved, a man hated by all who knew him and had to do business with him. However, there was an avalanche of lawsuits. Alleged lovers, illegitimate children, and deceived investors were all trying to take a chunk of the rock which Madeleine had earned when she'd stepped out of the chorus line at the Sands' "All Nude College Review" and into a marriage of misery. My job was to see that all of her rosebuds stayed exactly where she had gathered them.

"Buzz," she said as I approached the table. "The financial statements and will are all in this envelope." The envelope in her outstretched hand was almost hidden by the canary diamond, at least the size of a canary, which sparkled on one of her fingers. In fact, with the morning sun pouring in the bay window and bouncing off her gems, it looked like she was sending coded signals across the street— to Cartier and Dorfman's, perhaps, saying, "I'll be there."

I took the envelope from her.

"I'm sorry I can't stay, but I simply must leave town for a bit. The pressure has been appalling, and I'm going down to Mustique for a few days. Be a dear, have a nice breakfast without me and I'll call in a few days."

She stood up, brushed my cheek and walked out. I sat down, thinking what a great country this was. Not even de Tocqueville could have imagined that a semi-legit Las Vegas showgirl could, with enough money and time, morph into a woman of class and refinement. The words of her youth, "Buy a girl a drink," had become "Simply must" and "Be a dear." I looked around the cafe. How many more Eliza Doolittles sat nibbling strawberries and cream, the home fries of youth long forgotten?

The waiter came over and poured coffee. I ordered oatmeal in the spirit of an L.A. power breakfast. And what about me? A steady decline from marching to ban bombs to suing to save bimbos. Fortunately, I had an envelope full of documents. Introspection would have to await another day—or decade.

I read. I ate.

Breakfast finished, I rose to leave, and, looking out the window, saw Billy Bristol get out of a cab and head for the side door of the Ritz. I made a fast exit from the cafe so that I could bump into Bristol in the lobby. As I walked around the corner, the bellman was just saying, "Hello, Mr. Bristol. Nice to see you again."

I turned and there he was, my suspect numero uno. "Why, Billy, what a surprise."

"Well, Mr. Levin," he said. "Good to see that you are having breakfast these days. You'll need your strength. Isn't Barry's trial starting soon?"

Bristol appeared to be without a worry in the world. Dressed in a conservative but very natty blue suit, white shirt and red tie, he certainly didn't appear to be a dope-dealing murderer, although I'm not sure how central casting would want a man like that dressed. On the other hand, he was wearing brown wing tips, thus violating the classic admonition, "When in town, never wear brown." Sadly, this type of violation was not admissible evidence on the issue of character.

"Billy," I said. "You look like a man without a worry in the world. Will you be at the trial rooting for Barry and me?"

"I wouldn't miss it for the world but as for rooting, Barry needs a lot more than my good wishes."

"Who knows, Billy, maybe you'll be able to do more. Anyway, I'll leave you to breakfast." I tried to say this with a piercing glare. If I had succeeded in making him at all nervous, he certainly didn't look it. He started walking to a table, and I walked off to my car.

Up and down the street, shop doors were beginning to open. The space was too good to waste, so I fed two more quarters into the meter and walked across to Armani. I looked in the window and wandered through the store. My first experience with this designer was years ago when Ally and I were in Milan. After several draining shopping sessions, I had renamed the store "Ourmoney." But not today, Giorgio; I'm just looking.

I still wasn't ready for the office. Maybe I was too worried about Barry, but an existential ennui was creeping into my consciousness. Only some small conspicuous consumption could banish these clouds. What would Kierkegaard have bought on a day like this?

I wandered up Newbury to the corner and walked down Arlington Street. Hermes was always good for a therapeutic purchase. Camus was French. Maybe he went to Hermes whenever the benign indifference of the universe got too much for him.

I went into Hermes and went straight for the neckties.

"Bonjour, Monsieur Levin." It was my regular sales consultant who had held my hand through many a choice between ties with either little horseshoes, whales, birds, or butterflies. "Are you looking for anything special?"

"Not really," I said. "Just looking."

"Well, it's nice to see you again."

I picked up a tie that was covered with grapes but it didn't hold my attention. *Nice to see you again.* Where had I heard that? As I looked at a tie that had little silver clouds on a blue background, I remembered that it was the bellman at the Ritz who'd said those same words to Billy Bristol. A couple of the clouds started to lift and I knew I had to call in a quick subpoena. This was going to be fun.

I bought the tie.

A DECORATING TIP THAT'S FUN

Tapestry fabrics made into patchwork tablecloths are very fashionable.

THIRTY

S winging my new tie in its bright orange bag, I walked with a rejuvenated bounce and purpose back to Newbury Street and my car. Although I was downtown, I had no intention of going to the office. My practice was always to take a day off before a trial began. It was a lot like studying for exams in college. After days of busting one's ass to get ready for finals, a day of rest was necessary to let it all jell. So I hopped into my car and headed for the golf course.

If it weren't for days like this I'd have quit golf long ago. The sport is pleasant enough: walk around in the fresh air, hit a ball that's unlikely to hit you back (no such guarantees in other yuppie endeavors like squash or paddle tennis), and kibitz with like-minded layabouts. It is, however, the kibitzing that presents the real danger in the sport. The danger is that, if taken seriously, golf can overthrow an otherwise noble mind.

I've played golf with jurists, doctors, and philosophers. I've invited acclaimed scholars out on the links, people who should be discussing the great issues of the day. In one case, I invited a famous English professor to play with me, hoping that in our hours together he could improve my understanding of literary tradition. But when I

brought up Harold Bloom and the Western Canon, he only
wanted to talk about Arnold Palmer and the Big Bertha.
The trouble with playing golf is not so much the playing as
the talking. In no other sport do the participants spend so
many hours before, during and after recounting and
analyzing each of their shots. Every green is a source for
declamation. What begins pleasantly on the tee ends in
pure tedium.

I was lost in this antisocial meandering of the mind
as I made my way down Newbury Street, onto the Mass
Pike and out Route 128 on my way north toward the suburb
of Belmont. In fact, I was so lost in thought and, I must
confess, amazed at my own cleverness, that it didn't dawn
on me until I reached Route 2 and turned off of 128 that the
same car had been behind me since the middle of Newbury
Street. It was one of those pseudo-sporty cars like a
Firebird or something. All black, dark clouded windows,
and beginning to appear somewhat sinister.

Route 2 is a three-lane highway. I pulled into the
left lane and the car pulled right behind me. I swerved right
and slowed down. It mirrored my movements. I've seen
enough movies to realize that I was being followed; whether
by some joy-riding jerk or something a bit more evil
remained the unanswered question. It was, however, a
question I intended to leave unanswered. I decided to drive
the remaining two miles on the highway, take the turnoff
into the countryside and head for the country club
sanctuary. There was safety in numbers, and on a day this
beautiful there were bound to be numbers.

Constantly checking in the rearview mirror, I sped
up and headed for the turnoff with my shadow right behind
me. His windows were tinted and his face remained
obscure, but I could make out the outlines of his body. He
was very large, and largely familiar.

I took the Summer Street exit off Route 2. This was
a narrow winding country road that went on for a few miles

before reaching my safe haven. It was a picture-book-old New England way that ran between stone walls on both sides of the road. I figured that he couldn't pass on this narrow road and all I had to do was keep on driving. Midway through that brilliant figuring I felt a slam in the back of my car. My pursuer had driven into me.

I checked the rearview mirror and saw that he had pulled back. His car was built low to the ground for speed while my faithful Rover was built much higher, for safari. I could see that the whole top of his hood was smashed where he had driven into my rear tailgate. I smiled. Round one went to me and the overpriced Brits, but I still had a mile or so to go.

My concentration was broken when the rear window erupted. Every television watcher knows what that means, and it was not a happy realization. I was being shot at. I looked in my mirror and saw a head, an arm, and a gun sticking out the passenger side of the car. I cut back again, driving onto the side of the road as the street took a sharp turn. I looked around the corner and saw a fairway in the distance. Almost there. Parallel with the fairway, cutting across the road, was a large delivery truck lumbering my way. At almost the moment that I saw it, the van turned sideways, blocking the road. My speed was only forty miles an hour but I was headed straight for a very familiar Claridge and Sons logo on the side of the truck as I heard another shot from my rear.

Cut off from the front, chased from behind—but these brigands hadn't counted on the last vestige of the British Empire. I was sure Rudyard Kipling had the right line somewhere, but all I could muster was, "Tally fucking ho." I put the pedal to the floor and hurled man and machine to the left, off the road and up and over the stone wall. I'm no judge of hang time, but it seemed that machine and I were suspended long enough for Michael Jordan to have quadruple pumped before stuffing the ball. I held my breath as the Rover and I landed with a muted thud on the golf course side of the wall. Behind me, I heard the screech of brakes and collision of metal as my pursuer drove into his blocker. The crash was soft enough so that I knew no serious damage was done and a look behind me confirmed that the car and truck were trying to straighten themselves out on the road.

Suddenly aware that I still had the accelerator floored, I turned forward to see that the car and I were hurtling toward the eighth green, where a very surprised couple of golfers, Shirley Brightstein and her constant golf companion, Celia Bernstein, had looked up from their putting, saw the dreadnought bearing down on them, and were now running for their lives toward the rough. I slammed on my brakes, stopping at the edge of the green near the "No Carts" sign. I made a fast turn to the right and headed back to the road.

Fortunately there was an opening in the wall for golf carts to pass through as they crossed the street on the way to another hole. I kept it floored and skidded through the opening. I was on the road again. I looked back and saw that whoever they were had abandoned the chase and were heading back to the highway. The Claridge and Sons truck told me that my investigation had definitely struck a chord somewhere. But why would anyone want to kill me? That would only delay the trial until Barry got another lawyer. So it must have been delay they were after. Close down the deliveries, close out the fabric and the trail would quickly grow cold. But the heat was already on its way.

This victory on the road was actually exhilarating. I hadn't had time to break out in a cold sweat, which was sure to come later, probably in the middle of the night. *What the hell*, I thought, *no sense giving up on a brilliant day*. I headed for the parking lot.

I must have been visualizing Billy Bristol or Dr. Zaid or any possible number of malefactors every time I swung at the ball, because my game was at its peak. I almost broke ninety. I might have, except that on the eighteenth hole my adrenalized mental block finally gave way. I'd been chased and shot at. I was lucky to be alive. In the circumstances, a triple bogey was better than a funeral. I took a quick shower and headed home.

I called Peter from the car and brought him up to date. There were a few more things he needed to check up on for me. There were also some loose ends that we had left open, and I wanted them closed. I needed him to fly to Los Angeles and check out some of Bunny's history. Bristol was my prime suspect, but Bunny was still a stone we couldn't leave unturned.

I called Allyn and told her that I almost broke ninety. Although she gave no indication, I could sense that she was so quietly excited that I decided to spare her the rest of the day's events. I'd already faced death once, which was enough for one day.

I took the long way home, driving into town and across through Beacon Hill. Going by Louisburg Square, I noticed a parked car that was very out of place among the sedate Volvos and Mercedes station wagons. It was a black Firebird with a badly scarred hood and dented front fender.

THIRTY-ONE

L ife is full of big days: graduation, marriage, birth, the prom, getting a driver's license. For Barry, no day was going to be bigger than the start of his trial.

We were back at the same coffee shop across from the court where he and I had first talked. The trial was to start at 10 a.m., and we had assembled for a last minute pep talk. I was there with one of my bright young associates, Cindy Bingham, whose main tasks would be to keep track of the evidence, remind me about the law, and be a woman at the defense table. Last year, she was Editor of the *University of Pennsylvania Law Review* and today, she was going to be a prop. She was not only the best and the brightest, she was also a team player who was young and cute—we could be politically incorrect if it helped the cause. The help would come if I could get a few repressed ids on the jury to ignore damaging testimony and instead focus on dreams of satisfying Cindy. They could start by saying, "Not guilty." Some future sociology student would probably do a paper to demonstrate that the jury system was as reliable in determining guilt as colonial dunking stools. Perhaps, but I was out for a win, not eternal truth.

Barry looked very nervous, but also mainstream. For the last two days, he had been calling me about what I thought he should wear. I always find it remarkable how concerned clients are about what they should wear to court. Burglars, embezzlers, child molesters, armed robbers—they all think that what they wear to court is the key element of their defense, as if the right fashion statement would overcome the most damaging witness statement.

But, leaving nothing to chance, I always give the same advice: "Wear blue." Charles Revson was rumored to have owned five hundred blue suits. Blue was supposed to inspire trust while connoting importance. No one has ever been upset by blue. Barry looked positively all-American. He had made his first foray to Brooks Brothers, and the stylish Zegna that usually draped his torso was replaced with a basic single-breasted blue sack. I was slightly more upbeat in a blue Huntsman. Cindy had a very sensible Anne Klein blue suit.

Stromberg arrived a little bit late. He was wearing plaid, none of which was blue. I was prepared to forgive his sartorial gaffe if he had brought some informational bacon to breakfast.

"You're smiling, Peter," I said. "I assume this means more than just your pleasure at a free breakfast."

He reached out and grabbed a muffin, but, discovering it was sugarless bran, he quickly put it back. "Everything checked out, just like you thought," he said.

"Is there something we should know?" asked Cindy.

I stopped reading through the papers Stromberg had handed me and looked up. "I asked Peter to serve a few subpoenas and examine some financial records. The banking records are all confidential, so for these we only thank Peter without asking how he got them. As for the rest, if all goes according to plan, the case will never get to the jury. We should close this baby outright during the testimony."

"Oh, Buzz," said Barry, positively gushing, "do you mean I'm going to get off?"

Under the circumstances, I decided that even I should pass up the opportunity to jump on that straight line. Instead, I just gave Barry the thumbs-up and we ate a silent breakfast.

IN THE BEDROOM

Night tables should be twenty-eight inches high so that a lamp is at the proper position for light when you read in bed. Most tables are too low, so custom manufacture is your best bet.

THIRTY-TWO

Some lawyers believe that cases are won and lost in jury selection. There are research and opinion polling companies which can be hired to determine what types of individuals would be most sympathetic or hostile to your client. Sometimes the questioning of potential jurors can last longer than the trial, as attorneys delve into each individual's life history, hoping to root out or corral, depending upon the case, bigots, homophobes—even Republicans.

Massachusetts, sensible Yankee state that it is, doesn't believe in all these frills. Usually, only the judge questions the jurors, and lawyers have to rely on instinct to make challenges. Luckily, we were going before Judge C.D. Forman, who was bright and liberal enough to make sure that the defense got an even break. I was counting on him to allow me latitude in proposing questions to prospective jurors so that I could make some points which might seem irrelevant at the time.

The courtroom was crowded with reporters, assorted onlookers and potential witnesses. The galleries were far more upscale today than at the usual Suffolk County felony proceeding. Without knowing what was going on, someone walking into the room might have thought that a Palm Beach divorce was about to begin. There were decorators and Women's Leaguers, trust fund babies and society hangers-on. Billy Bristol was there, as were Willie and Patsie. Bunny was there by herself. I looked around for Ashworth and saw that he was sitting in the back with Ally. Frankie was near the front and Johnny at the back. Even Megan was there. She was in a wheelchair, accompanied by a nurse, but she appeared as out of touch with reality as she had been since the incident.

Across the aisle was my opposition. Unlike the bail hearing, the D.A. himself was appearing. Johnny Boyle was a career prosecutor. He was all Boston, a triple Eagle— Boston College High, then Boston College, then Boston College Law School. Suffolk County was still an Irish stronghold and with the right jury he could make his closing arguments sound like "Danny Boy." He was also first in his class and he liked to win.

The Judge entered, the bailiff intoned the Hear Ye's, and we were off.

"Good morning, counsel. It appears that we are ready. Bailiff, please bring in the first panel."

Given this direction, it was the bailiff's job to go down to the jury pool and come back with thirty or forty prospective jurors. Sitting in the jury pool, a room on the second floor, were about two hundred people, most of whom would rather be elsewhere. Sixty days ago, they had received notice that it was time for them to enjoy the fruits of democracy and show up for jury duty. And now a group was walking into the courtroom.

"Ladies and gentlemen," began Judge Forman, "when you were downstairs in the jury pool, Judge Singal told you about the case of Commonwealth versus Stapleton. As you remember, Judge Singal excused some of your group for various general reasons. I'd like to ask you some specific questions, the answers to which may affect your ability to serve. I'd like the lawyers to stand up and introduce themselves to the jurors."

We did.

"If any of you know these lawyers or knows anything about them that would affect your impartiality, please step forward so that I can speak with you."

No one did, and Judge Forman proceeded. "I'd like the defendant, Mr. Stapleton, to stand up and face the jury. If any of you know Mr. Stapleton, please come forward."

Again there was no response and the judge continued. "If the clerk will please read out the fourteen numbers, we'll start picking our jury."

Seated in front of the judge's bench, the clerk had on his desk a large canister on a spindle. It is similar to the rotating drum used by bingo callers to mix up the numbers before making a choice. And, just like in a bingo game, the clerk gave the canister a twirl, reached in and started calling off numbers. Each member of the jury pool had been assigned a number and as each was called he or she moved from the spectator's seats to the jury box. As each number was called, I pulled that juror's sheet from in front of me to match the name with the numeral. Boyle and the prosecution team did the same.

The juror sheets gave name, address, occupation, and spouse's occupation. The only other information contained on the page came from a requirement that each juror list whether any family member had any connection to law enforcement. Among the group of fourteen were a file clerk at a Wal-Mart, three unemployed housewives, two retirees, a mailman, a flight attendant, a legal secretary, a computer programmer, a night watchman, a graphic designer, and a woman on welfare. I studied the group and studied my sheets. Hunches and bias were all I had to go on. I would have loved the chance to question each of them to determine their prejudices. As this process was not allowed in Massachusetts, I had to rely on my own prejudices.

The file clerk was an Irish kid from South Boston. The Supreme Court had just upheld the right of South Boston parade organizers to keep gay groups from marching in the St. Patrick's Day parade. He may have been one of the unwanted marchers, but I had to play the odds. He was out. The legal secretary was a sure scratch from my list. I knew the office she came from, and if she was as cynical as her boss, I didn't want her to sit in judgment of my client. Those two challenges would be peremptory, meaning that I didn't need a reason. The flight attendant would be for cause. Her husband was a Charlestown cop. I looked at her. She looked back, smiled and shrugged.

Boyle got rid of the welfare mother. I guess he assumed that she was mad at someone, and probably the police. The graphic designer had no chance on his list.

The five that we challenged were replaced by the pulling of five new numbers. These were a clothing salesman, milk delivery man, two more housewives, and a mechanical engineer. I bounced one housewife whose husband was a retired marine; too much respect for authority. She was replaced by a social worker who was immediately challenged by Boyle. A taxi driver took her place and was acceptable to all. Fourteen people—twelve jurors and two alternates—became the group of peers who would decide Barry's fate.

In a criminal trial, the prosecution goes first. Their side has the burden of making an opening statement and proving a case without the participation of the defendant. Our side need do nothing. And so I sat at my table, hands folded, looking expectantly at Boyle, who rose to address the jury. He was a large, imposing figure, with a big shock of white hair. Like most good theatrical lawyers, he carried no notes and paced up and down in front of the jury rather than stand at the lectern.

"Ladies and gentlemen of the jury," he began, "an opening statement is a promise. It is my promise to you of what the evidence will show. I intend to keep my promise and I intend to prove Barry Stapleton guilty beyond a reasonable doubt...."

From there he launched into a concise recitation of the evidence as we all knew it. Anticipating the defense's arguments, he acknowledged that the case was circumstantial. "No one saw the hammer come down or the garrote tightened," he intoned. "Criminals don't always work in front of an audience. But the evidence in this case is so overwhelming, so damning of that man," he said, pointing at Barry, "that you are the only audience justice needs to bring down the curtain on this killer." A little corny for my tastes, but the gang of fourteen seemed ready to applaud.

"Do you wish to open, Mr. Levin?" Judge Forman asked, looking my way as Boyle walked to his seat.

"I'll reserve, thank you." I needed the element of surprise for my plan to work, and there was no requirement that I open.

"Members of the jury," the Judge began, "Mr. Levin has chosen not to address you at this time. That is his absolute right and you are to infer nothing from his silence. Call your first witness, Mr. Boyle."

"The Commonwealth calls Rebecca Church Whitney."

Ms. Whitney, Becca to her friends, was first on Boyle's witness list and I was well prepared for her. I assumed Boyle wanted to use her for her Show House background. I had other plans.

The woman who stood in the courtroom and walked toward the witness box looked like a caricature drawn to fit her name. She was tall, probably five-eleven, even in the simple flats she sported. Her blond hair was etched around her face in a New England Puritan evocation. Her skirt was beige, blouse pink. Her purse was a whale-bone ditty box scrimshawed with the obligatory Nantucket wildflowers.

She walked to the box, was sworn in, and sat, ditty box on lap, with hands folded.

"Good morning, ma'am," began Boyle as he rose from his seat. "Would you tell the court your name, please?"

"Rebecca Church Whitney." She sat ramrod straight and smiled as the name rolled off her lightly lipsticked lips. She was, of course, delighted that she could begin with her name, thus drawing the attention of all to her exalted rank in Boston society. No doubt she counted on the general mediocrity of public education that failed to emphasize the role of her forebear, Dr. Frederick Church, during the American Revolution. Although less sung than Benedict Arnold, he was the first significant British spy, who regularly reported to General Gage on the doings of Revere, Adams, and his other fellow members of the Sons of Liberty. Clearly, old money had dulled old memories.

"Are you associated with the Boston Women's League and their Show House?"

"I'm the President, and the person ultimately responsible for all of the activities."

From that point, Boyle used the witness to describe the League and its many good works. She talked about the Show Houses and how they benefited designers while raising money for the League. Boyle showed her pictures of the Show House so that she could give the jury the flavor of the murder scene. She even identified Allyn's room as the work of the defendant's lawyer's wife. I assume this was an attempt at guilt by decorative association. By the time she'd finished, the jury had received a nice overview of the total Show House environment. Boyle finished his questioning and walked by me with a smile and a nod. I'm sure he assumed I would have few, if any, questions. I smiled at Boyle, winked at Cindy and walked toward the witness.

"Tell me, Mrs. Whitney, what is the purpose of the Women's League?"

"We are a charitable society. The Boston Women's League was organized after the War of 1812. One of my ancestors was its first president. I'm very proud of this heritage and I strive to honor it." This last statement was said with an abundance of condescension. No doubt she harbored the belief that descendants of the Daughters of the American Revolution had a leg up on the scions of Sons of the Shtetl. We'd see about that.

"And please tell the jury some of the current charitable works of your group."

"With pleasure. We've just laid the cornerstone for a new research lab at the Children's Hospital. We distribute food to the homeless and clothing to poor families. We are building a group of hospices throughout the city."

"Truly wonderful, Mrs.Whitney. Now tell me," I said as I paced slowly in front of the jury, "I assume these good deeds cost a good deal?"

The mere mention of money caused the aristocratic nose of the witness to turn up, as if in the presence of some foul odor. "I assume so." She looked at me as if I were the source of the offense.

"The buildings, the food, the charity. These are substantial works. How do you pay for all of this?"

"Well Mr. Levine,"—she mispronounced my name so elegantly I saw no reason to correct her—"we have a number of fund-raising events. There are bake sales, rummage sales and, of course, the Designers' Show House."

"How much do you raise from these events?"

"I really wouldn't know. You see," she said, crossing her legs and elegantly smoothing her skirt, "I've never really had too much to do with money. Isn't that why God created trust officers?" She looked at me with a simple smile.

Walking back to the defense table I extended my hand and Cindy passed me a pile of papers.

"Mrs.Whitney, isn't it true that the large charitable projects you described have only been going on for the last two years?"

"I suppose so."

"In fact," I said, waving the papers around, "isn't it true that three years ago your organization was almost disbanded because you were having difficulty raising money?"

"We don't like to air our dirty laundry in public, sir."

"This will be just a short breeze. Your old and honorable organization had been mismanaged almost to the point of bankruptcy, isn't that correct?"

I saw Boyle out of the corner of my eye. He was rising and I beat him to the punch. I turned to the judge.

"This may seem a little far afield, Your Honor, but I can tie it all up."

Judge Forman waved his arm at me dismissively and I continued.

"What's the answer, Mrs. Whitney?"

"I'm afraid that's true. But as you can see, sir, we've certainly turned things around."

"Exactly," I said. "But how?"

She sat up, beaming. "I really don't know the details. But Patsie Winthrop and Willie Potts, two of our devoted members, offered to serve as co-treasurers. They said they had a plan. I guess they did."

"Are those women in the courtroom today?"

"They most certainly are." The witness pointed out Patsie and Willie, who appeared less than thrilled with the high praise they received.

I walked up to the witness box and handed the papers I was holding to the witness. "I'd like you to look at those documents I have just given you. These are bank statements I've subpoenaed. They show all of the deposits into the Women's League checking account for the last two years. Have you ever seen them before?"

"No."

"Do you see on each page where it lists deposits for each month? Please look at these pages and tell me whether during the first week of each month a rather large deposit is made to the accounts."

Mrs. Whitney looked down at the sheets and then up at me. She seemed to be a bit flushed. "You'll just have to help me, Mr. Levy, I've never seen a bank statement before."

The audience laughed, the judge gaveled, and I approached the witness.

"See that number right there? What does that say?"

"One million dollars."

"And if you turn the pages and look at each page, how much money do you see in every month?"

"One million dollars."

"Twelve million dollars a year. That's a lot of bake sales."

The witness had regained her composure and her disdain was flowing again. "I really wouldn't know."

"Who would?"

"Well, I guess you'll just have to ask Patsie and Willie."

I turned around and faced the audience. "I guess I will." Turning back, I looked toward the witness. "No further questions."

As Rebecca Whitney stood to walk out of the courtroom, she passed by Willie and Patsie, who were staring straight ahead, looking unhappy.

"Your Honor," Boyle said, standing by the prosecutor's table. "If that last witness was any indication, it appears that Mr. Levin is going to drag this case out for weeks." Here he turned and nodded toward me, thus indicating that at least Boyle knew the difference between Levin, Levy and Levine. She had probably called him Sullivan when he interviewed her. "It looks to me like he's trying to confuse the jury with meaningless lines of questioning."

Judge Forman looked down from his bench. "Well, Mr. Boyle, this is a murder trial, after all. And I will afford the defense considerable latitude. But I'm a bit puzzled myself. You didn't make any opening statement, Mr. Levin, and that was your right. But I don't think it inappropriate for me to ask how many witnesses you plan to call."

I smiled. The pitcher had floated one right down the middle. Our defense wasn't great but this weak hitter had just been given the changeup of his dreams. "I'm not sure how long I'll take, Your Honor." Looking out at the audience I continued. "I plan to call my investigator, Mr. Stromberg, as well as Billy Bristol, Patsie Winthrop, Willie Potts, a Dr. Zaid, and a few people known only to me at this time by their jobs, not their names." Before anyone had a chance to react, I added, "Those would be the head concierge at the Ritz Carlton Hotel, the bookkeeper at Claridge and Sons, the bookkeeper for the Women's League, and the dispatcher at Dante's Divine Pizza. I believe they're all here."

Judge Forman looked somewhat dubious. "Are we part of the same case? Come to sidebar."

Boyle, Cindy and I walked up to huddle at the bench. Judge Forman stood and leaned over to us. "Mr. Levin, I would never interfere with a defendant's case, but who the hell are all those witnesses?"

Before I could answer, I detected some movement out of the corner of my eye, and I looked out to the room.

All of my witnesses were standing, and my hoped-for denouement appeared to be moving on schedule. Patsie and Willie were next to each other. If they had put on any makeup this morning, the effort was in vain. Their once delicately rouged cheeks had turned alabaster. Their pearls looked colorful when compared to the frozen faces that hung over them.

If they were frozen, however, Bristol was not. Movement began at the top of his head and worked its way down. First, his eyes flicked from side to side as if he were sitting paralyzed at center court and an active volley was in progress. At one point, they stuck upon the concierge from the Ritz, who waved to Bristol. This seemed to set the rest of his body in motion and he began, with feigned nonchalance, to ease himself out of his bench row into the aisle. Patsie was on the other side of the aisle and the sight of Bristol starting to leave must have caused some sort of neuron overload. Her face reddened and she screamed out, "You're not leaving, you son of a bitch," and jumped into the aisle, tackling Bristol.

Judge Forman stood up and banged his gavel, yelling for order. Unfortunately, various budget cutbacks in the Commonwealth had reduced courthouse security. A greater problem was that, because of seniority rules, all of the young, athletic bailiffs were home watching talk shows, leaving two unenthusiastic quasi-pensioners at the door.

Luckily, Bristol didn't look too closely at these guardians of order. He shrugged off Patsie and, after taking a couple of steps toward the main door, reversed his course and started running toward the front of the room.

Now Willie was in action, and she jumped on Bristol, clawing at his neck. Like a wild animal driven by pure adrenalin, Bristol struck out, thinking only of survival. From the inside of his coat pocket he pulled out long scissors, which I knew from my decorative background to be drapery shears. Then he wheeled around and stuffed them into Willie's stomach, who went down in a heap, blood gushing.

Bedlam reigned. There were screams as jurors and spectators rushed for the door. Others fled into the aisle and surrounded the fallen Ms. Potts. The doors to the back of the courtroom opened. The police had arrived, but they made no progress entering the room because of the hysterical occupants who were running out.

Bristol stood alone, bloody shears in his hand. He looked up at the bench and the intensity of his wild eyes focused directly on me. "You're dead, Levin. Dead!" he screamed as he rushed forward. "I never got to kill Bruno, but now I'm going to kill you."

Bristol hurtled the bar enclosure and was coming our way, not running now but deliberately walking. *What were the odds,* I wondered, *one demented killer with drapery shears facing three lawyers armed with Mont Blanc pens?*

It was then that Judge Forman proved his mettle and reminded us all of what a great third string quarterback he had once been in his University of Pennsylvania days. As Bristol made his charge, only a few feet from us now, Forman reared back and threw his gavel. Although not a spiral and certainly not a pass that would ever have brought the crowd to its feet at the Franklin Field, it hit Bristol squarely on the top of the head.

Bristol seemed stunned and for the moment stood straight and frozen, shears by his side. It was then that I did what I've been waiting to do ever since I saw my first Western. I stepped forward, and with all the force I could summon on such short and unrehearsed notice, gave the old one-two—a left to the jaw and a right to the nose. He dropped like a falling curtain. A policeman jumped on top of him and handcuffed him. I don't know if it was my delivery or Bristol hitting his head on the floor when he fell, but he showed no signs of regaining consciousness in a hurry.

While Bristol was immovable, the rest of the room moved like a supercharged atom. People were jumping up and screaming. In the melee, I saw the back of Dr. Zaid as he walked through the crowd and out of the room behind the human wedge of Alfred. There was such confusion trying to aid the wounded and arrest the guilty that Zaid was gone before I could call for help.

Amidst all the confusion, Judge Forman started yelling for order. We all made our way back to our seats as the paramedics carried stretchers holding Willie and Billy out of the courtroom.

"Well, Levin," the judge intoned, looking down from his bench, "I've never been a fan of theatrics in the courtroom, but this looks more like *Saturday Night Live* than Court TV...Boston Women's League, pizza guys, dirty money—it doesn't get any better. But son," he said, beckoning me over, "we're still trying a murder case here. The guy didn't confess. I can hardly wait to see how the esteemed District Attorney is going to deal with a high-class charitable organization that raises money in most unusual ways—especially in an election year—but I've got to keep this case going. We'll take off a few days, but the case goes on."

To say I was crestfallen and distraught was an understatement. But things weren't calming down enough for a more detailed introspection. All eyes turned toward Megan, who was suddenly energized from the attention and stood up from her wheelchair.

"Who decorated this room?" she demanded from no one in particular as she waved her arms around the courtroom. "Just look at the placement of those chairs. It looks like a jury box, not a living room. I've got a lot of work to do; a lot of work." And here she looked around the courtroom until her eyes focused on Ashworth. She looked straight at him, let out a piercing wail and slumped back into her chair and fell asleep.

We all looked at Ashworth, who shrugged his shoulders and sat back down.

Judge Forman, after pausing for a moment, shook his head to clear the fog. "Here's what we're going to do. Levin, it seems to me that your theory of the case just turned to manure. But you've done the Commonwealth a great, albeit unintended, service, although I can't quite figure out what it is yet. So I'll do you a favor and allow you to regroup. I'm declaring a mistrial. Before we start again, we'll take some time and see where this all shakes out. Court," he said standing up and walking off the bench, "is in recess."

THIRTY-THREE

The courtroom began to clear and I was left at our table with Barry, Peter, and my defense team. Bunny came over. "I just wanted to congratulate you, Buzz. This was the most awesome trial I ever saw."

"Thanks, Bunny. But I still can't figure out what happened."

"I'm sure you'll come up with something," she said, leaning toward me for a quick kiss on the cheek. "I wanted to say goodbye. I'm going back to L.A., without Steve. He's a little too much and I've got to get back to my life."

"You know, Bunny," I said, "Megan's attack is still an open question. Maybe you shouldn't leave town."

"I'm not worried," she said as she walked away, turning back just to add, "oh yeah, I remembered the answer to the question you asked."

"What question?"

"You know, the bathroom...at the hospital? I remembered that it was Steve, because not only did he have to go, but he took so long I figured he really did have to go. Well, 'bye."

"'Bye yourself," I said, turning to Stromberg. "Have you seen Ashworth?"

"He was in the back with your wife. I think they walked outside together."

"I've got a very bad feeling about this. We may have missed all the signs, but I think Ashworth attacked Megan. Maybe he also killed Bruno. There's a decorator he used before Megan who vanished a couple of years ago, and now, in the midst of this crisis, he's off with Ally."

"Oh, my Lord," said Barry.

"There's a serial decorator killer on the loose and he's got my wife. C'mon!"

Barry, Stromberg and I raced down the hall and out of the building. The sidewalk was empty. I was starting to panic. Stromberg saw a court officer and ran over to have him call the police. When he returned, I was no calmer.

"The police will put out an APB. They can't have gotten very far."

"Well, I'm not just sitting around. I've got to do something. Ashworth keeps a suite at the Four Seasons Hotel. Let's go." And the three of us dashed off to a cabstand on the corner and headed across town to the Four Seasons. We arrived in three minutes, which seemed like three years, and ran into the lobby.

I went over to the front desk. "Is Mr. Ashworth in?"

"Why yes, sir. He and his lady friend just went up to his room." The clerk looked around and leaned over the desk toward me. "Very nice, too, if you catch my drift. A bit older than his usual, but quite nice."

I grabbed the clerk's tie and pulled him toward me. "Listen, you asshole, that's my wife—she's no date, she's a victim. Call the police."

"Sir," he said, straightening his tie, "I suggest you take your domestic problems elsewhere."

Stromberg stepped in. "I suggest you give us the room number and call the police, or your health will take an immediate turn for the worse."

"606."

We dashed for the elevator and got off at the sixth floor. Amazingly, the door to 606 was open, and the three of us carefully entered. My heart sunk when I saw that he was holding Ally, one hand around her neck, the other hand holding a knife-like object under her chin.

"Don't come any closer, Levin, or your wife dies."

"Steve," I said, "don't do anything stupid."

"Stupid, stupid...it's a little late for that now. The stupidest thing I ever did was to think that this bitch," he spat as he pulled her tighter, which caused a slight gasp from Ally, "was any different than all the others."

"Keep him talking," whispered Stromberg out of the side of his mouth.

"Others," I said.

"Fucking A, others," he said with a wild gleam in his eye. "One disappointment after the next. Never quite right. Never my vision. Megan, she was the worst. I wouldn't set foot in my house when she was through with it. That's why I came to Nantucket. Fresh start, fresh decorator. Hah! When I heard that Megan got her head bashed in I was thrilled."

"What do you mean, 'When you heard'?"

"That's right. You think I tried to kill her? Not me, pal. Well, not the first time, anyway. I liked the idea of her being dead so much that I tried to kill her in the hospital. Bad luck. It was even worse luck the last two times I tried to kill your wife. Two Show House tries and two misses. But I think my luck is about to change. You know what they say, third time's a charm."

While Ashworth was talking, Ally had managed to give herself a little breathing room. He must have noticed and pulled her closer, looking back and forth at us and then her. Finally making a decision, he dragged her into the bedroom. We followed, but he stopped us at the door. His back was to the open window. "Come another step closer and I stab her and throw her out the window," he said.

He was crazy and beyond reason. We had to do something. The failure of my second theory as to who killed whom was of no consequence. I whispered to Stromberg, "Now you keep talking to him." So Peter and Barry struck up a conversation with this lunatic while he stood with what now appeared to be a Four Seasons letter opener held to my wife's neck by an open window six floors above the street. My only inspiration was to sneak up on him from behind. At least that way I might be able to grab Ally if he tried to push her out the window. So I eased myself out onto the window ledge and, step by step, slid along toward the bedroom window.

I had seen ledge-walking in the movies, where it always looked like something that was made harder than it really was for comic effect. Trust me, it wasn't easy and it wasn't comic. I only looked down once. Good news: My old friend Lt. Daley was getting out of a car with a bunch of other cops. But he was going to be too late, which made for the bad news: I was Ally's only hope.

I reached the bedroom window just as I heard Ashworth winding up a long harangue.

"That's why she has to die. That's why they all have to die." And as he yelled "Die, decorator, die!" my world stood still and the following happened: holding Ally away from his body, he pulled back his arm with the letter opener to get more leverage to stab her; I reached forward to grab his arm, but missed and grabbed his ponytail instead; I yanked back on the ponytail causing him to yell in pain, loosen his grip on Ally and fall out through the window.

I was so intent on pulling him away that I never loosened my clutch on his hair, even as he hurtled through the window and started to fall. So there we were falling through space—Ashworth holding a Four Seasons Letter opener, me holding Ashworth by his Hollywood ponytail, and Ashworth still screaming, "Die, decorator, die!" Fortunately, I landed on an awning that extended out over the front door. Even more fortunately, Steve, who was falling to my right, just missed the awning. When I looked over the side, I saw him lying on the sidewalk, a letter opener wedged in his head. And then I realized that when I fell, I had my hands extended in front of me, and in landing probably broke both of my wrists, which were already weakened from punching out Bristol. This explained the pain, and the fact that as I lay there trying to figure out who the original murderer was, I passed out.

THIRTY-FOUR

I spent the rest of the day at Mass. General. Cindy was nice enough to wait for her fallen leader and drive me home. Ally was there, but she was so shaken up and so worried that Justin would be worried if he heard the news that I sent her home. She was amazed when I asked her to invite certain people to the house for cocktails. She argued that I was in no shape for a party; but while lying in the hospital with nothing to do but think and rethink, I had another idea—with any luck, better than the last few. So I insisted, and told her to do the same when she invited people.

Both my hands were in casts from fingertips to above the wrists. Cindy had to open the car door for me and buckle my seat belt. I began to think of all the things I wouldn't be able to do for myself. Perhaps Cindy had the same thoughts, as she seemed in an unusual rush to get me home and unload me. It seemed as if I had just closed my eyes when we pulled into the driveway. She repeated her tasks and helped me out.

The front door was open and Ally and Justin were standing at it, clapping as we walked forward.

"Dad, it was on all the news stations. You're a hero."

Did I detect a lack of teenage nonchalance?

"Aw shucks, pilgrim," I said in my best John Wayne. "It wasn't nothin'."

Ally hugged me. "You were better than John Wayne. You were Clarence Darrow and Superman, all rolled up in one."

My two heroes, there was no better praise. I put my arms around her and let my hands drape low across her back. I had all sorts of plans for my hands until I remembered that they were currently encased. I touched her nose with the tip of my left pinkie.

"That's it for about three weeks," I said.

"We'll think of something," she countered. "Come on, the gang's all here. *Why* is beyond me, but here they are."

I walked into the living room. Barry and Stromberg were both there. Cindy was mixing herself a drink. I looked around and saw that Lieutenant Daley had shown up, as had Bunny, Johnny, and Frankie. We all said hello to each other.

"Make me a very dry martini, will you Cindy?" I asked. "And bring me up to date."

"Well, boss," began Stromberg, "Ashworth is still dead. Daley showed up just in time to see you save the day, not to mention the missus."

"You'll be interested to know," Daley said, "that I called and spoke with the LAPD. They've started reinvestigating the disappearance of Ashworth's old decorator. On top of that, it seems that five years ago Ashworth had a home in Cannes where his French decorator was found washed up on the beach one morning. It was classified as an accident; they'll look at that again, too."

"This is all very well and good," said Barry. "And I don't want to rain on your parade. It's no mean trick to break up a drug ring, solve some old murders, and save your wife, but what about me? I'm still on trial for murder."

"I've been thinking about that, old boy. You know, it does look bad. You had the means, the motive and the opportunity. Sort of the Tinkers to Evers to Chance of crime."

"Please, Buzz, stop joking," Barry said, turning as crimson as the shirt he was wearing.

"It's no joke," I said. "You're still the prime suspect. But then again," I continued, turning to the other people in the room, "I wonder if you're as good a suspect as, say, a woman who was driven nearly insane by the suicide of her father."

All eyes shifted to Bunny. "So insane that she blames Megan, who was having an affair with her father, for causing his death. Depressed, she comes to Boston where, quite by accident, she sees Megan. And she sees that Megan is deliriously happy in what looks like an affair with Bruno. That young woman is so unhappy that she wants no happiness for Megan or anyone associated with her. She wants only death."

Bunny cried out, "Buzz, it's not true! It's not true!" I had an urge to tell her that it was and I was "sending her over." But it wasn't, I wasn't Bogie, and this wasn't *The Maltese Falcon.* So I turned around and stared at Frankie and Johnny, who were standing together.

"She's right. She didn't do it. But as I laid in that hospital bed, it dawned on me that I'd seen all the clues, but I'd missed their meaning. Nope, Billy didn't do it, and neither did Ashworth, nor Bunny, nor, I'm happy to say, did Barry."

"Enough already, Dad. Who did it?"

"Good question, Justin. I think the person who did it wasn't crazy or jealous; his driving force was old-fashioned greed. He was involved in a series of dubious transactions and Bruno found out. Bruno was as greedy as his killer and demanded money to keep quiet. That demand sealed his fate. That's it, ladies and gentlemen," I said, turning around with a flourish and pointing with my hand covered with a cast. "Lieutenant, arrest that man!"

It was a great moment, but because my hand was virtually encased, pointing was impossible and no one could figure out at whom I was pointing.

"Which one?" asked Daley.

"Why Frankie, of course."

"You're crazy," Frankie said. "You've had too many painkillers. You've got nothing on me."

From the way my audience was reacting, it seemed that they might have agreed with him. I continued, "The numbers are all there, Frankie, and they all add up to 'You did it.' Bruno figured out your scam of over-ordering fabrics and then selling off the excess. At first, it seemed like penny ante stuff, until Ally told me your workroom has a national business. The numbers could get very large. Bruno probably figured that out and demanded a share of the cash."

"Cha-ching," said Barry.

"Exactly. Then you learned that Bruno and Megan had become close. They were seen everywhere and you wondered whether Bruno had told Megan about you. You became certain of that the night you, Bruce and Rebecca saw Bruno and Megan at a club. I remember Bruce saying that Megan pointed at him and laughed. But Bruce misunderstood. It was you they were pointing at. Megan wasn't laughing at Bruce's absurd get-up, she was laughing at how she and Bruno were going to stick it to you."

"You can't prove any of this," Frankie said, with more bluster than conviction.

"Sure I can. There were only two clues at the murder scene. First, the fabric around Megan's head. It was a new line that hadn't been released to the public yet. At least that's what Ally thought and that's why I thought Bristol must have done it. But then I learned that some of this decorator stuff gets released in L.A. before it gets to Boston and, better still, that you were working on the West Coast for Ashworth and probably some others as well.

"The way I see it, you were looking for a chance to get to Megan or Bruno. One night, you followed Megan into the Show House and just by chance the fabric that you grabbed out of your car to go along with the hammer is the one that debuted on the West Coast and, I bet, was used at Ashworth's. The next morning, you were at the Show House. Ally saw you. You used the confusion surrounding Megan's discovery to go upstairs looking for Bruno. You found him, and that time your weapon of choice was a tassel chord. Who else but a drapery person would carry a tassel chord in his pocket? You killed him, ran down the back steps and rejoined the crowd. With Megan non compos mentis and my boy Barry in the can, you thought your troubles were over."

"Oh, my God," said Johnny, as he slowly sidled away from Frankie. "Are you sure?"

"Sure enough to bet that this guy is so cocky that there's a blood-stained hammer in the trunk of his car and that Ashworth's West Coast house has that fabric on its window treatments. Shall we look?"

All eyes looked instead to Frankie, who'd slumped into a chair. "You don't have to look. It's there. You're right."

Again my hand shot out à la Paul Muni. "*J'accuse.* Arrest that man."

Which is just what Daley did. He arrested him, handcuffed him and read him his rights, all in my living room. I could tell Justin was thrilled. Then Daley led Frankie out, and the rest of us were left in silence.

The silence lasted for about a moment, when Barry suddenly burst out in tears of joy. He tried to kiss Stromberg. I let him hug me.

"You did it, Buzz," said the exuberant Barry. "I knew you would. How can I ever thank you?"

"You can start with that martini." Barry handed me the glass and I discovered that the stem fit perfectly in the plastered slot next to my thumb. I took a sip.

"But, Buzz," he began, "how did you do it?"

My second magic moment of the day: "Elementary, my dear Watson."

"Do we have to humor him?" Justin asked.

"He's injured, Justin. We'll be nice to him for another couple of hours," Ally responded.

Undaunted, I persevered. "You heard my logic. That's all you need. Logic and, of course, luck. What if he'd thrown the hammer away? Never discount the importance of luck."

"But what about Patsie and Willie, and this whole Women's League drug thing?" asked Cindy. "I still can't figure out how you tied them in."

"That was the best part. I had my partner, Sam, make some inquiries among his blue-blood clientele. It seems that Patsie and Willie were heroes to the Women's League. Until two years ago, the League was in serious financial trouble. Their Show House events weren't making much money and the League couldn't keep up its own mortgage payments, let alone support any charitable work. It was becoming one huge embarrassment. Then, all of a sudden, money started to roll in. People wondered how things got so good so fast, but no one cared because Patsie and Willie had saved the day."

"Incredible," said Ally. "The Women's League was dealing drugs. From rum and slaves to cocaine in five generations. Go figure."

"I guess they figured the ends justified the means. Let this be a historical lesson to you, Justin. Anyway, I had Stromberg explain our theories to the League and the owners of Dante's Pizza. They agreed to cooperate and show up at the trial. At that point I still had no absolute proof that all of these tied together, but I figured that if I listed all the witnesses as if I could prove something, someone might crack. When Boyle called Whitney as his first witness, my scenario started to play. I solved the crime; I just didn't know at the time it was the wrong crime."

"Where did that Arab doctor fit into all of this?" someone asked.

"I assume that he was the money man who got the whole thing going. It takes tremendous capital to get started in the drug business. Zaid is probably one of the world's dirty international bankers. The Boston operation was so lucrative, he was probably setting up a base here. By the way, what happened to him?"

Stromberg replied, "He snuck out of the courtroom during the fight. The police found his name on a flight manifest to Geneva. They checked the house and it had been cleaned out. Nothing left but the furniture."

"What do you think will happen to Megan?" asked Ally.

"When I was waiting at the hospital, I asked some doctors about her," said Cindy. "They don't expect her to ever be mentally sound enough to stand trial for anything. She'll get off, but I wonder what she'll do."

"Mental soundness was never a prerequisite for interior design," I said. "She'll probably stay in business. With a reduced IQ she can do minimalism."

"The heck with her," said Ally. "What about me? This is becoming a hazardous profession. There's officially been a serial decorator killer. Who knew decorators were so unpopular? What are we, lawyers?"

"Maybe we can start a line of decorator jokes," said Justin.

"Maybe, but first a victory dinner," she said.

"You've been cooking?" I asked incredulously, holding her back as everyone else walked to the dining room.

"Do you think I'd serve pizza or Chinese food to my champion? I made an all-American meal for my all-American hero: Steak and lobster."

"This may be a bit difficult," I said, raising my encased and immovable hands. "I'm going to have to count on the kindness of strangers, not to mention family, to eat for the next few weeks."

Ally put a hand into my back pocket and alternately guided and massaged me toward the dining room. "For now," she said, smiling at my martini and increasing her massage, "why don't you stick to olives for dinner? I've got something special in mind for dessert and you'll never notice your hands."

And she did.

And I didn't.

Later that night, when I closed my eyes, I heard a crowd cheering. I was standing near a race track. It looked like a scene from the Kentucky Derby. I was walking into the winner's circle, but there was no horse, just me. I felt something heavy on my shoulders and discovered that a wreath made of hundreds of roses had been put around me by someone. I turned to see who it was, and there was Clarence Darrow.

He had a mint julep and raised it in my direction.

"Nice job, kid," he said. "You almost won."

"What do you mean, almost?"

"Did you get paid?"

"Get paid!" I yelled. "That's all I ever hear from you, 'Get paid...get paid.'"

And then I felt a warm body against me, and a tongue in my ear. "Whatever you say, Buzz," whispered Ally. "I don't have to start the Nantucket Show House for another two days."

A FINAL WORD

Fabrics in a room should coordinate, never match.